KERIS STAINTON

SPOTLIGHT ON SUNNY

For Iffath, Fatima and Lily

CATNIP BOOKS
Published by Catnip Publishing Ltd
320 City Road
London
EC1V 2NZ

First published 2015
1 3 5 7 9 10 8 6 4 2

Text copyright © Keris Stainton, 2015
The moral rights of the author and illustrator have been asserted

Cover design by Tim Rose

A CIP catalogue record for this book is available from the British
Library

ISBN 978-1-84647-187-2

Printed in Poland

www.catnippublishing.co.uk

1

'You'll phone us every day,' Sunny's dad said, squeezing her against his chest. She could feel her hair vibrating where his mouth rested on the top of her head.

'Yes, I've said I will,' Sunny said. 'Please don't wipe your nose on my headscarf.'

Her dad laughed. 'I'm not crying. Why would you think I'm crying?'

'Because I know you are,' Sunny said. 'Even though you promised you wouldn't.'

She stepped back, freeing herself from his grip. He totally was crying, tears were dripping off his jaw. She handed him one of the tissues she'd brought for exactly this reason and he blew his nose.

They were standing in the middle of the station concourse, people rushing around them, the PA system announcing trains. Every time the automatic doors opened, they could hear a busker singing Beatles songs.

'It'll be fine,' Sunny said.

'I know, I know,' her dad said, nodding. 'It's just . . . I'll miss you. We've never been so far apart.'

'You've been to Bangladesh without me!'

'Oh, that's true,' he said and smiled sheepishly, 'And you must keep your phone on at all times. You can put it on silent if you have to, but don't switch it off. And if me or your mother phone, you have to answer –'

'If I'm in class –' Sunny interrupted.

'Unless you're in class. But only then. Otherwise . . . you answer.'

'Right.' Sunny nodded.

Her mum and sister came back from M&S, where they'd gone to buy her some food for the journey. Her mum handed her a carrier bag, then kissed her on both cheeks and gave her a hug. Sunny relaxed into the embrace. It had been a while since her mum had hugged her properly – she wasn't very physically affectionate, not with Sunny anyway. Sunny inhaled the scent of her. She smelled like home.

Sunny's sister Aisha hugged her quickly and said,

'Have a great time. Be careful. London is very busy and fast.'

'I know!' Sunny said. 'I have been there before, you know.'

'Yeah,' Aisha said. 'For, like, a day.'

'Don't stay up too late,' her mum said. 'You need your sleep.'

'Don't get into trouble,' Aisha added.

'Of course she won't get into trouble!' their dad said. 'This is Sunny. She's a good girl!'

They all stood looking at each other and Sunny felt a lump forming in her throat. These people drove her completely nuts, but she loved them so much.

'Hadn't you better get back to the car?' Sunny said. The small station car park had been full, so her dad had left their car on double yellow lines on the main road. He said it would be fine, her mum worried they'd get a ticket, Aisha said she had told them they should have got the ferry over.

'No, we're okay!' her dad said. 'We'll wait until your train.'

'You don't have to,' Sunny said. 'Honestly.' She had visions of them waving hankies, her dad running down the platform, the other passengers laughing at him.

'We're not leaving you here on you're own!' her dad said.

'I won't be on my own,' Sunny said, spotting Hannah and Kitty crossing the concourse towards them. 'Look.'

Hannah and Kitty arrived, dropped their holdalls next to Sunny's and greeted Sunny's family.

'Your parents didn't want to come and see you off?' Sunny's mum asked them, frowning.

'My mum's working,' Hannah said.

She pulled her blond hair out of its ponytail and fastened it up again. She always did that when she was nervous. Sunny was reassured to find that Hannah was nervous too.

'My dad had to work as well,' Kitty said.

'How's your mum?' Sunny's dad asked, doing the sympathetic head-on-one-side thing Kitty hated, although she didn't mind it from Sunny's dad so much.

'Much better, thanks.' She tucked her short dark hair behind her ears. 'She's in remission. She's hoping she can go back to work part-time at my sister's school in September.'

'Oh, that's wonderful,' Sunny's mum said.

They all stood smiling at each other. They heard a

snatch of the busker singing about hiding your love away.

'So I'm going to go and get a drink,' Hannah said, pointing at the nearby Costa. 'Anyone want anything?'

'I was going to get one too,' Sunny said.

'Maybe we should go back to the car . . .' her mum said, looking at her dad. 'We don't want to get a ticket.'

'We won't get a ticket!' her dad said. He stared at Sunny, tears welling in his eyes again.

'Tissue,' Sunny said, smiling.

'I will miss you, my sunshine,' he said. 'And don't worry about what we talked about –'

Sunny hugged him, saying, 'No, it's okay. It can wait till I get home.' Then she said a quick bye to her mum and sister and practically ran to Costa.

'Can you believe they wouldn't let me come on my own?' Sunny said. The three of them had bought their drinks and were sitting outside the café, on the station concourse.

'Of course they wouldn't,' Hannah said. 'I thought they'd want to come all the way to London with us. You know, to make sure the accommodation was okay.'

Sunny pulled a face. 'They've looked at it online. And dad has spoken to everyone involved. And I mean everyone. He's been phoning at different hours to catch different people. He called at 5am and spoke to one of the cleaners.'

'He's just protective,' Kitty said. 'It must be hard for them.'

Sunny rolled her eyes. 'They talk all the time about me going to university. Mum actually booked for me to go and visit one. And that's four years off. They can't wait to get rid of me.'

'That's not true,' Kitty said. 'They're just proud of you.'

'They have to control eveything! And the rules about my phone. What did your mums say?'

'Mine said, "See you in three weeks. Don't get in any trouble",' Hannah said. 'I said, "I probably won't get pregnant!" but she didn't notice. She was on the computer.'

'Gah, Hannah,' Sunny said. 'Way to make me look bad.'

Hannah grinned at her.

'Dad woke me up this morning so we could have

breakfast together,' Kitty said. 'He wants me to phone every night, but he knows I probably won't.'

'I think I'll just not phone Mum and see how long it takes before she notices,' Hannah said.

Their train was announced over the PA and the three of them grinned at each other.

'This is going to be so great,' Sunny said, draining the last of her hot chocolate.

'I know,' Hannah said. 'London, baby!'

2

'Bagsy top bunk,' Hannah said, throwing her bag up on to the bed.

'You can't bagsy it!' Sunny said, looking round the room that was to be theirs for the next two weeks. It was nice. Plain, but nice. And much bigger than she'd expected.

'Why not?' Hannah said, hands on her hips.

'You just can't.'

Sunny headed over to the window and looked down at the street below. The building was university accommodation during the school year, but the rooms were often rented out during the summer, both to tourists and for summer courses. They were on the fourth floor so there was a great view of the Strand. Sunny watched the red buses and black taxis on the road down below and grinned to herself.

'Well, do you want it?' Hannah asked. 'The top bunk?'

Sunny turned back from the window and wrinkled her nose. 'No. But Kitty might.'

'You're fine,' Kitty said. She was already hanging stuff up in the wardrobe nearest to the bed Hannah wanted. 'Have it, Hannah.'

Hannah said, 'Yay!' and climbed the ladder to sit on the top bunk next to her bag. She crossed her legs, rested her elbows on her knees and her chin on her fist and said, 'So. London. Where first?'

'You heard where first,' Sunny said. 'Get unpacked, then go and meet the other students for orientation.'

'Then dinner and then free time,' Kitty finished, pushing her fringe back out of her eyes and her holdall into the bottom of the wardrobe.

Hannah flopped back on her top bunk, making the mattress creak. 'I want to go to the London Eye. Or Piccadilly Circus. Is it too late for us to do a bus tour?'

'You're as bad as my parents,' Sunny said. 'The only time they brought us to London, it was like a military operation – they marched us on and off buses and in and out of the Tower of London and we didn't have any time to just hang out. Can't we just hang out a bit?'

'But I don't want to miss anything,' Hannah said. 'I

don't want to spend two weeks in London and just see the dorm and the school.'

'Let's go and meet everyone now and then later we can walk down to the river maybe,' Sunny said. 'I don't think it's far.'

'It can't be as far as it was to get here and we managed that okay,' Hannah said.

Their train had arrived at Euston and their tickets included travelcards so they were able to get the tube straight away. All the information and directions had been in the pack that had been sent out to everyone taking the course. Sunny's dad had been over and over it with her – it was the bit he was most worried about. He'd kept telling her that London could be confusing and overwhelming when you first arrived, but she hadn't been worried because she had Hannah and Kitty.

And he was right, Euston *had* been overwhelming – so much noisier and busier than the station they'd left – but it had been easy to find the tube, and only a few stops on the Northern Line to Charing Cross. From Charing Cross it had been a short walk along the Strand to the dorm where they were staying.

The Strand had also been busy and noisy, but Sunny hadn't really taken it in – she was too busy looking out for the building and making sure she didn't lose Hannah or Kitty and that they all kept hold of their bags.

At the dorm, they'd been met by a guy named Steven, who had shown them to their room and told them about the meeting, dinner and free time. He also told them they weren't to leave the building without speaking to an adult first and that if they failed to return to the dorm when requested or if they missed curfew, they wouldn't be allowed out unsupervised again. Sunny didn't think this sounded too unreasonable, given their age, and she knew her parents would approve.

'Are you two going to have a shower?' Hannah said. 'I can't be bothered.'

'I don't think we've got time,' Sunny said. 'I'm just going to clean my teeth.'

She lifted her holdall up on to the desk between the two large sash windows at the end of the room and unzipped it, taking her washbag into the en-suite bathroom. The bathroom was white and very bright with shiny tiled walls, a grey rubberised floor like you get in hospitals and an almost dazzling overhead light, which was presumably to make up for the bathroom not having a window.

Sunny smiled as she looked at herself in the mirror that took up the full wall behind the basin. She couldn't quite believe she was in London on her own. Well, not on her own – with her best friends – but away from her family. She was going to meet new people who knew nothing about her and she was going to have fun and learn about film-making. With her friends. And, as her mum had pointed out repeatedly, have something to put on her university applications. In four years' time.

She frowned at herself, grinned and then – excitement bubbling up inside – came close to laughing out loud. And then, worried she was losing it – giggling at her own reflection – she tucked everything back in her washbag and zipped it up.

Back in the bedroom, Sunny unpacked the rest of her bag while Kitty and Hannah took turns in the bathroom. Sunny lifted out Caspar, the teddy she'd had since she was a toddler, and gave him a quick cuddle. He smelled reassuringly like home. Aisha had told Sunny not to take a teddy. Begged her not to, in fact – said she'd be humiliated on Sunny's behalf, even from a couple of hundred miles away. But there was no way Sunny would have left him behind. She'd never slept without him and even though she was excited to be away from home, she suspected she might get lonely and homesick too.

But she did tuck him between her pillow and the wall, so you couldn't see him from the rest of the room.

3

'I'm Steven Perkins, but you can call me Steve. Or Steven. What I mean is, you don't have to call me Mr Perkins. You're not actually at school now. Also, I'm not a teacher. Well, I am. But I'm not one of the teachers on your course. I'm more of a chaperone.'

Sunny, Hannah and Kitty were sitting on the front row of chairs that had been set out in the common room on their floor. Like their bedroom, the common room had huge windows looking out over the Strand. They were all open slightly and Steven (or Steve) – who kept fiddling with his watch strap and pushing his rimless glasses back up his nose – was having to almost shout over the sound of the traffic.

The sound of the traffic that was giving Sunny butterflies. It sounded so vibrant and exciting out there. She wasn't like Hannah – she really didn't want to just go out and discover stuff, she was happy to wait and be accompanied – but it was hard to wait. Because it sounded awesome. And a bit scary.

Steven told them about the various classes that were available to them – writing, producing, directing, acting, CGI animation, even how to choose props and costumes. Most of the classes were taking place at a building in Covent Garden, but there would be optional trips to studios, particularly for anyone interested in animation.

'So the first week is about getting a feel for all the different aspects of film-making,' Steven said. 'By the end of the week, you'll have your favourites and then in the second week you'll create your own short film, which will be judged by the staff. You might want to start thinking about getting yourselves into groups – usually of three or four – and you'll need to be thinking about who's going to do what – writing, filming, sound, etc. Obviously you'll get a clearer picture of that when you've had some classes, but it's something you can be thinking about in the meantime. And then on your last night –' he paused for effect – 'we have an Oscars-style award ceremony.'

The girls grinned at each other.

'But without the budget!' Steven added.

'It sounds great,' Kitty whispered.

Sunny nodded.

'And now to the bit where you all boo me,' Steven said, leaning against one of the window ledges, his skinny legs crossed at the ankles. 'We want you to have as much freedom as is realistic . . . But obviously we have to keep you safe.'

No one booed, but a few people groaned, including Hannah.

As Steven ran through the course's 'code of conduct', Sunny looked round at the other students. There were about thirty of them and, same as at school, Sunny was the only one wearing a hijab. There was another Asian girl, but her head was uncovered and her hair was in a huge bun. She was fiddling with her nose-ring and her fingernails were long and pointy. She was sitting next to a white boy with a huge blond quiff and a Japanese girl with thick glasses and a backpack on her lap. The backpack had a spiky dinosaur spine running down the centre. Sunny smiled and turned back to look at Steven, who was saying that alcohol was not permitted at any time and that they would have a curfew.

'Everyone has to be back in the building by 9pm,'

Steven said. 'Lights out is at 10.30pm and this will be strictly observed.'

That time someone did boo and everyone laughed.

Steven wrinkled his nose to shift his glasses back into place. 'London is tiring – you need to sleep.' He cleared his throat. 'On this side of the lift we have the girls' rooms –'

One of the boys – Sunny thought it was the one with the quiff – whooped.

'Yes, that's exactly what I was about to say,' Steven continued. 'No boys in the girls' rooms and vice versa. We usually have boys and girls on different floors, but we're a smaller group this year and so . . . But, no. You can –' he took his glasses off and put them back on again – 'mix in here. That's fine. But not in the rooms. Okay? Staff members will be staying on this floor. Me and Liz, who you'll meet later, I hope . . .' He took his phone out of his pocked, frowned at it and put it back. 'And anyone caught breaking the rules is risking being sent home early. Does anyone have any questions?'

'What do we do for food?' a tall skinny boy who was wearing headphones – one on one ear, the other on the side of his head – asked.

'Good question,' Steven said. 'Food is available in

the canteen downstairs or you can cook in here, if you want to, but we do ask that you clean up after yourselves, no one wants to be doing anyone else's manky dishes. It would be best if you didn't cook anything too smelly, so no curries.' He glanced at Sunny. 'Or fish or anything like that. And no food in your rooms.'

'When is the canteen open?' Hannah asked.

She'd been complaining she was starving since they checked into their room. Even though she'd been eating all the way down on the train.

'Ah, well,' Steven said, smiling. 'Because it's your first night, we've got a special treat. We're ordering in pizza.'

Some of the other students cheered and Sunny was pleased too – she'd been a bit worried that the food would be like at school or that they'd all have to chip in and make it together or something. Even as a one-off, pizza was a good start.

She was already convinced that the course was going to be fun.

4

'Do you think the curfew is just an official thing and they'll be more relaxed unofficially?' Hannah was saying as they walked back into their room.

Sunny shrugged. She hadn't known for sure there was going to be a curfew, but she'd assumed. And it was fine with her. One of the things she'd been concerned about was that the course would end up being a two-week party with no one doing anything useful. She'd actually lost sleep worrying about it. She only had a couple of weeks there and she wanted to learn as much as she could. About everything.

And then she heard the loo flush.

'Is someone in here?' Kitty said.

Sunny's stomach flipped as she noticed that Caspar – her teddy – was on top of her holdall on the desk. And that another bag was on the bottom bunk, which had been Sunny's bed.

'I think we're sharing with someone else,' Sunny said, pointing at the bag.

'Oh great,' Hannah muttered, climbing straight up the ladder to her bunk and taking out her phone.

'I thought it was just going to be us,' Kitty said, frowning.

Sunny crossed the room and tucked Caspar back in her bag, zipping it up. She didn't want the top bunk. She'd just tell whoever this girl was that she was scared of heights, or something.

The bathroom door opened and a girl came out wearing just her bra and knickers. And flip-flops. And she was completely gorgeous.

'Hey,' she said. 'Were you guys at the meeting?'

She had an Australian accent.

Sunny nodded. She actually took a step back and bumped into the end of Hannah and Kitty's bed.

'Sorry I nicked your bed?' the girl said, pulling her long blond hair into a ponytail. 'I can't sleep on the top, sorry. I've had labyrinthitis?'

Sunny didn't know what that was. She looked at Kitty, but Kitty shook her head, she didn't know what it was either. Hannah was leaning forward, holding on to the bunk-bed railing and frowning, her mouth slightly open.

The girl opened her holdall, which wasn't a boring black canvas one like Sunny's – it was bright pink and looked like leather. She took out her washbag then sprayed deodorant under her arms. Sunny put her hand over her mouth.

'I'm Danielle?' the girl said, turning round.

She was smiling at them like this was completely normal. Her teeth were straight and dazzlingly white. Fourteen-year-olds couldn't get their teeth whitened, could they? That was mad.

'I'm Kitty,' Kitty said.

'Hannah,' Hannah said. 'And that's Sunny.'

'What's labyrinthitis?' Sunny asked.

It was the only thing she could think of to say, but she immediately felt stupid. Why couldn't she just have said hello like a normal person?

'Oh,' Danielle said, waving her hand. 'It's this really horrible thing in your ear. It makes you dizzy? And sick. I felt like I was falling all the time, you know? I had to have an operation and they took a bit of my ear out. I'm okay now.'

'So why can't you sleep on the top bunk then?' Hannah said. 'If you're better, I mean.'

Danielle smiled. 'I just can't, sorry. It freaks me out. I can't do heights now. And I don't think it's gone completely, anyway. Like, I felt dizzy coming up in the lift just now?'

She pulled a pair of jeans out of her bag and wriggled into them. Actually wriggled, they were super tight and had frayed rips and holes all down the thighs. Sunny had to look away.

'Were you guys at the meeting?' Danielle said again, pulling a vest top over her head. 'I'm never on time for anything. Can you catch me up?'

5

Sunny, Kitty and Hannah crossed the common room and sat down at one of the large tables at the back. The tables were the same kind they had in the cafeteria at school – long, grey plastic things with rounded edges and graffiti scratched into the surface.

Hannah and Kitty sat down on one side and Sunny sat opposite, her back to the room. They'd waited for Danielle for a bit, but she'd gone into the bathroom with a make-up bag as big as Sunny's washbag and didn't show much sign of coming back out any time soon, so in the end Hannah had knocked on the door and said they'd see her later.

The tables started filling up with other students. A very pale girl with long blond hair and a terrified expression sat next to Hannah and stared down at her phone. A boy with dark skin, black-rimmed glasses and a hoodie that said *I waffle therefore I am* sat next to her.

'I'm Hannah,' Hannah said to the blond girl. She

looked up from her phone, her eyes wide, and said, 'Sophie.'

'Have you done this before?' Hannah asked her.

She shook her head. 'I've never been away from home before.'

Her voice was so quiet that Sunny had to strain to hear what she was saying.

'We've got a film-making club at school,' Sophie said, biting her thumbnail. 'There's five of us that've come. What about you?'

'We won a competition,' Hannah said.

As Hannah told Sophie about the competition, the waffle guy introduced himself to the table in general. His name was Joel.

'Sunny,' Sunny said and smiled at him.

He held his hand up to acknowledge her, but then someone he knew came and sat on his other side and he turned to greet them instead. The new boy introduced himself as Dillon.

'Kitty's girlfriend's called Dylan!' Hannah said, grinning.

Kitty rolled her eyes and Sunny wondered if Kitty was okay with Hannah outing her to people. It wasn't something they'd really talked about yet.

'Oh yeah?' Joel said. 'You're gay? That's cool.'

Kitty laughed. 'Yeah. It's very cool.'

'So is your girlfriend, like, here with you?' Dillon said.

Kitty shook her head. 'No. It's just me, Hannah and Sunny.'

Dillon leaned forward, looked at Sunny and did one of those upwards nods before turning straight back to Hannah.

'And what about you? Boyfriend not with you?'

Hannah giggled. 'No, I left him at home. And he might not actually be my boyfriend any more anyway. Haven't decided yet.'

That was news to Sunny. She looked at Kitty and, from the look on Kitty's face, figured it was almost certainly news to Kitty too.

The table filled up, but the seat next to Sunny stayed empty.

When Steven came over and put two enormous pizza boxes down on the table, Sunny swung round on her chair and looked at the rest of the room. All the other seats were taken. Except for the one next to her.

'Looks like I'm sitting with you,' Steven said, pulling out the chair next to Sunny's.

Sunny saw Hannah smirking at her and she

frowned back. Typical. No one wanted to sit next to the girl with the hijab. Great.

'So who's the other teacher?' Hannah asked Steven as she pulled a slice of pizza out of the box.

They all watched as the cheese strings stretched right across the table and then snapped back like elastic bands.

'Liz,' Steven said. 'She was supposed to be here earlier, but she . . . got held up.'

He coughed then reached for his glass of water.

Hannah grinned across the table at Sunny. Sunny knew Hannah would be coming up with all sorts of nefarious explanations for Liz's lateness.

'What happened?' Hannah asked. 'To Liz?'

Steven shook his head. 'It was a . . . personal matter. She should be here soon though. She never usually misses pizza.'

He took an enormous bite of his own slice of pizza, presumably to prevent him from answering any more questions.

'So you'll both stay here?' Kitty asked.

He nodded and pointed to his mouth.

'And you'll come with us on trips and stuff?' Hannah said.

He nodded again.

'But you're not one of the actual instructors, are you?' Sunny said. Just for something to say really. She was pretty sure he'd told them that earlier.

Steven swallowed. 'No. Liz and I are sort of chaperones. That's all. The film school has its own staff. We're just here to keep you all, um . . .'

'Out of trouble?' Sunny said.

He nodded, smiling. 'Yes, exactly. More pizza?'

He picked up the other pizza box and swapped it for the one that had been in front of them.

Kitty and Hannah each took a slice, but it was pepperoni, so Sunny couldn't eat it.

'You're not having any?' Steven said. 'Sorry, I don't know your name.'

'Sunny. No, I don't eat pepperoni.'

His cheeks flushed. Sunny actually saw the red run up and then down his face.

'Oh, I'm so sorry,' he said. 'I didn't even think.'

He reached across the table and pulled the original pizza box back over. Joel was just taking a piece and frowned at them.

'You can eat this okay?' Steven said to Sunny. 'You can eat . . . cheese?'

Sunny nodded. 'Yeah, it's fine. Thanks.'

She took another slice, even though she didn't

really want it. But he'd gone to the trouble of getting it for her so she felt like she had to.

Sunny was about halfway through it and Steven hadn't said anything – he seemed to be too embarrassed to speak – when a woman came over and stood at the end of the table. She was tall with long dark hair and quite a pinched, serious face.

'Sorry, sorry,' she said to Steve.

'Hey!' he said and jumped to his feet. 'That's okay. Did you get it sorted?'

The woman – presumably Liz – nodded. 'Everything good here?'

'Yeah, great, fine.' He moved around the table to stand next to her. 'Do you want to sit down?'

Liz shook her head. 'No, I'm going to go and sort out my room, if that's okay? You can cope here?'

'Yeah, I think we're pretty much done.'

He introduced Liz to Sunny, Kitty and Hannah and then once she'd gone, taking a slice of pizza with her, he went to talk to some of students on another table.

'They are totally doing it,' Hannah said.

'Do you think?' Sunny said. 'Why?'

'He was all shifty about when she was going to get here. And then they didn't look at each other properly.'

'Maybe they don't like each other,' Kitty said, grinning. 'Maybe they're mortal enemies.'

'Nah,' Hannah said. 'Totally doing it.'

'Well, they can't do it here,' Sunny said. 'Cos they have to stick to opposite ends of the floor.'

'Oh, Sunny,' Hannah said. 'So naive.'

Sunny stuck her tongue out at her. 'You ready to go back to the room?'

'No!' Hannah said. 'Let's go out! I'm asking Steven.'

Kitty and Sunny headed for the door, but Hannah grabbed them and pulled them across to Steven and asked him. He looked unsure.

'We just want to walk down to the river,' Hannah said. 'We'll come straight back, promise! It's only five minutes away, isn't it?'

'It's not far, no,' Steven said. 'Look, let me get your numbers.'

He got out his phone and they all gave him their mobile numbers and took his.

'Ring if you need anything at all,' he said. 'And be back here by eight.'

'I thought it was nine!' Hannah said.

'It'll be nine tomorrow if you make it back tonight by eight,' Steven said.

6

They waited for the lift for a while, then gave up and walked down the fancy stairs with the iron bannisters, black-and-white tiles and huge windows, then pushed through the double doors out on to the Strand.

The noise and smell of the traffic hit them straight away and it took Sunny a few seconds to get used to it, particularly after the cool quietness of the dorm building.

'When are you seeing Tom?' Hannah asked Kitty as they waited for the lights to change so they could cross the road.

Kitty's brother, Tom, was at university in London.

'I said I'd phone him tomorrow, after we've had the classes and everything,' Kitty said. 'He said he'll come up and take us out for dinner. I'd better tell Steven, actually, make sure it's okay.'

'All of us?' Sunny asked.

Kitty nodded. 'He's got a new job that pays better

than the last one. He's going home at the weekend. He said he'll be able to go up every month or so now.'

'That's great,' Sunny said. 'Your mum'll be pleased.'

'She's really excited,' Kitty said. 'So's Dad. He's got activities planned for the next year or so, I think.'

They crossed as far as the middle of the road and waited while three red double-decker tourist buses went past.

'This is mad,' Sunny said. 'I can't believe we're really here. It's just so . . . London-y.'

'Do you remember when we came in Year 6?' Kitty said, starting to laugh. 'My mum nearly had a nervous breakdown.'

Sunny and Hannah laughed too. Kitty's mum had come with them as a helper and had spent the whole time worrying that she was going to lose someone else's child.

'She counted us so much that she said she was still counting in her sleep when we got home,' Kitty said. 'She only volunteered to go cos she didn't want me going on my own.'

'Aw, that's sweet,' Hannah said, bumping Kitty with her shoulder.

'I still can't believe my parents let me come,' Sunny said.

Hannah and Kitty looked at each other. 'Nor can we,' Hannah said.

'I think Aisha talked them into it,' Sunny said. 'Which way is it?'

The three of them looked around, then Hannah said, 'Excuse me?' to a man wearing a suit and carrying a big black portfolio. 'What's the quickest way to the river?'

He didn't even speak, just gestured down the gap between the bank they were standing in front of and the pub next to it.

'Okay then,' Hannah said. 'Friendly!'

A woman pushing a buggy turned off the Strand and walked down there, so they figured it was okay for them to go too. Once they were through the gap they saw it was a real road – a narrow one – and they could see trees at the bottom, so they assumed it was the right way. The buildings were tall so the road was in the shade. Sunny shivered, glad she was wearing long sleeves and not T-shirts like Hannah and Kitty.

Halfway down the road, they passed a truck where some men in high-vis jackets and hard hats were replacing some paving stones. One of them whistled.

Sunny ignored it, deliberately not even looking in their direction, but Hannah growled. 'I hate that. So creepy. You whistle at dogs, not people.'

'I don't even get it,' Kitty said. 'What's it supposed to mean? Are we supposed to be so impressed that they can whistle that we'd want to go out with them?'

'And then you find they can only whistle, not talk,' Hannah said, grinning. 'Actually I might prefer that with some boys.'

'What was that you were saying about Louis?' Sunny said. 'At dinner.'

Hannah pushed her blond hair behind her ears. 'I don't know. He's been doing my head in.'

'I thought you were all in lurve,' Sunny said.

Hannah wrinkled her nose. 'No. Well *I'm* not anyway. Don't know about him.'

'Did the big goodbye not go well?' Kitty asked.

Hannah pulled a face. 'He kept going on about other boys on the course and what would I be doing and who would I be doing it with? And I said I didn't know who else was on the course, but he couldn't expect me to keep away from all boys in, you know, London. And he got a bit of a gob on.'

They crossed the road.

'I mean, we haven't split up or anything,' Hannah said. 'He texted when I was on the train saying he trusts me, which is a bit rich coming from him.'

'What about Dylan,' Sunny asked Kitty. 'Was she okay with you coming away?'

'Yeah, she was fine,' Kitty said. 'We're going to Skype and everything.'

'And everything?' Hannah said, grinning at Sunny.

Kitty rolled her eyes. 'She's helping my gran's WI out with their charity bunting thing tonight anyway.'

'Sexy,' Hannah said.

At the bottom of the road a black wrought-iron gate led into a park.

'That must lead to the Embankment, right?' Sunny said. 'Or do we have to go round?'

'Might as well try it,' Hannah said.

They crossed over, went through the gate and found themselves in a wide and almost-empty park.

'This looks like our park,' Sunny said, pointing to a rose garden with paths through the middle.

'No bandstand though,' Kitty said.

They walked right through the middle of it − the gardens were full of huge, tropical-looking plants with spiky leaves and bright red flowers − and out through the gate at the other side and suddenly they were on the Embankment, looking across at the Royal Festival Hall and the London Eye.

All three of them fell uncharacteristically silent – although they probably couldn't have heard each other speak over the road noise anyway – until they'd crossed over and were standing at the wall, looking down at the river.

'This is fantastic,' Hannah said.

Sunny nodded. 'I can't believe we're here. I know I've said that already, but . . . I can't.'

'Remember when we learned about the Thames in History,' Kitty said. 'The Great Stink? How people died from the smell of the river?'

'The river was full of boats . . .' Sunny said.

There were a few boats now – a couple of tourist cruise boats, some people actually kayaking – but most of the river was clear.

'And rubbish,' Kitty said. 'And dead bodies.'

'It's kind of like being at home,' Sunny said. 'Standing looking across the river.'

Hannah laughed. 'It's not quite the same. This one is in the middle of the city. Our river has the city on the other side. And way more dog muck.'

'It's still nice though,' Sunny said. 'Sort of makes me feel at home.'

'I know what you mean,' Kitty said and hooked her arm through Sunny's.

7

They walked along the Embankment as far as Westminster Bridge, where they all stood and watched the London Eye for a while.

'We've got to go on it, obviously,' Hannah said.

'They'll probably do a trip on the course,' Kitty said.

'I want to go to the Houses of Parliament,' Sunny said. 'Do you think they do tours?'

Hannah stared at her. 'We're in London. Why on earth would you want to go there?'

Sunny shrugged. 'I think it would be interesting.'

Hannah shook her head. 'We'll be learning stuff during the day on the course. Once we're free, we should be having fun.'

'Learning is fun,' Sunny said.

Hannah pretended to scream.

'You don't have to come with me!'

'Too right!' Hannah grinned.

The three of them walked across Westminster Bridge, weaving around all the tourists taking photos with the London Eye or Big Ben in the background.

'We should do that,' Kitty said.

'Not that,' Hannah said, pointing to a guy in a vest and short shorts, holding his iPhone out on a stick to take a selfie.

'Ha, no,' Sunny said. 'But we should definitely take a photo.'

'London Eye or Big Ben?' Kitty asked.

'London Eye,' Hannah said, just as Sunny said, 'Big Ben.'

'We'll do both,' Kitty said. 'London Eye first.'

They leaned back against the green wall at the side of the bridge – Kitty in the middle, Sunny on the left and Hannah on the right, holding her phone at arm's length. Hannah said, 'Cheesy!' and they all grinned.

'Crap,' Hannah said, looking at the photo, most of which was of her thumb. 'I don't think my arms are long enough.'

A boy stopped and said, 'Want me to take it for you?'

He was only about their age. Brown-skinned with a cropped afro. Very cute. And in a wheelchair.

'Yes! Great! Thanks!' Hannah said, handing him her phone.

'I always worry when people offer,' he said, looking at the phone and then holding it up. 'In case they nick my phone. But you know I'm not going to do that. Hang on . . .'

He started to stand up.

'No no! Don't get up!' Sunny said, reaching out to take the phone off him.

'It's fine, honest,' he said. 'I can stand.'

He held the phone out, took a photo and then said, 'I'll just take another one. You all look a bit startled.'

He grinned and they laughed. He took another photo and looked at it. 'That's a good one. You're on the film course, aren't you?' he said, handing Hannah her phone back.

'Yes!' Sunny said. 'How did you know that?'

'I'm on it too,' he said. 'I'm Will.'

Sunny didn't want to say that she hadn't seen him. That would be rude. But she hadn't.

'You didn't see me,' he said, the corner of his mouth quirking in a smile.

'Sorry, I –' Kitty started.

'It's okay,' he said. 'So where are you from?'

They told him as they headed back towards the Strand and the dorm. He told them he lived in Brighton and he'd had to wait for his mum to come back from work to drive him up today.

'She can be a bit overprotective,' he said.

'My parents are like that too,' Sunny said. 'I didn't think they'd let me come at all.'

'So how come they did?' Will asked.

They turned the corner off the bridge, passing a statue of Boudicca and a stand selling postcards, flags and fridge magnets.

'We won a film-making competition,' Sunny told him. 'The three of us. It was just a short thing for the local tourist board, but the prize was to come on the course. So I think they felt like they couldn't really say no.' She smiled. 'My mum still tried though.'

'Mine did too,' Will said. 'She was worried about me being in London on my own. But, you know, I have to do stuff on my own sometimes. She can't always look after me.'

'Is it just your mum?' Hannah asked him. 'Not your dad?'

'Yep,' Will said. 'My dad left when I was four. I still see him, though, he only lives about five minutes away.'

'I've just got my mum too,' Hannah said.

The lights changed and they crossed the road, hanging back on the other side for Will to get his chair up the kerb.

'I never knew my dad,' Hannah said.

'That sucks,' Will said.

Hannah laughed. 'Sometimes, yeah.'

'I think it was my dad who talked my mum into letting me come,' Will said. 'He's all about independence. Which is probably why he buggered off.'

Sunny, Hannah and Kitty laughed and Will grinned at them.

'So are you three sharing a room?' he asked.

Sunny told him they were. 'Except there's another girl as well. We don't know her.'

'She just turned up and nicked Sunny's bed,' Hannah said.

Will pulled a face. 'I've got my own room. An accessible one by the kitchen. Tiny window.'

'Ours has got huge windows, but a rude Australian girl,' Hannah said.

'Ohhhhh her,' Will said. 'She was in the kitchen when I arrived. I thought she seemed . . . confident.'

Sunny laughed. 'Yeah, she's definitely that.'

They turned into the park and Will said, 'Hey, this is great! I didn't come this way before.'

Sunny felt her phone vibrate in her pocket. She knew it was probably her dad, wondering why she hadn't phoned. She'd ring him when they got back to their room, like she promised.

8

When they arrived at the dorm, Sunny headed to the prayer room. On the way, she couldn't help noticing that the other rooms had their doors open, music was playing and people were shouting and laughing. Either Steven had relaxed the rules for everyone for the first night or he'd totally lost control of the situation already.

Back in their room, there was no sign of Danielle and Sunny was relieved. She hadn't even considered that they might have to share with a stranger – she was glad she hadn't thought of it because if she had she'd have been dreading it – and it was really putting a dampener on things. She'd been looking forward to hanging out with Hannah and Kitty, her best friends for years, who knew her well and understood her. She really didn't want to deal with anyone else in their room, not when they were going to be getting to know new people during the day.

'Am I okay to have first shower?' she asked Hannah and Kitty, pulling her hijab off and hanging it up in the wardrobe.

'Fine by me,' Hannah said. She was lying on her top bunk, her iPad propped up against her pillow.

'I'm ringing Dylan,' Kitty said from the bunk below.

Sunny took her holdall into the bathroom with her and put it behind the locked door. She never really trusted doors, sometimes locks were loose. At least this way if anyone did come in they'd trip over her bag.

There was nowhere else to sit apart from the loo, so she put the lid down, sat on it and got out her phone to ring her dad. But the message wasn't from her dad. It was from Sam. She grinned and opened the text.

Get there okay? Not lost on a tube?

And then there was a second text, also from Sam.

The Tube I mean. Not a tube. That would be weird.

Sunny started typing.

Did you know the tube is an actual tube? It's Boris Johnson's job to squeeze the end to make the trains run.

She put the phone on the side of the sink while she cleaned her teeth. It buzzed almost immediately.

I wondered what his job was :) You got there okay?

Sunny replied that yes, they had and yes, it was good so far. She finished getting ready for bed, expecting another message, but her phone was quiet until just as she was about to go back into the bedroom. And it was her dad, asking why she hadn't rung. She felt like an idiot. She couldn't believe she'd forgotten to ring on the very first day. She wouldn't be surprised if her dad demanded she come straight home.

She pressed the button to call his mobile and he answered before she'd even heard it ring.

'I'm sorry, I'm sorry,' she said.

'I wasn't worried,' he said. 'But your mother is very upset.'

Sunny grinned. She knew it couldn't be too bad, if he was coming out with that. Both of her parents always claimed it was the other parent who was upset.

'I'm sorry,' she said again. 'We had a group meeting and then dinner and then a few of us went for a walk.'

'With a teacher?'

Sunny crossed her fingers on her right hand. 'Yes. Steven. He's kind of in charge at the dorm. He's nice.'

'How is your room?'

Sunny described the room, the bathroom, the dorm, the pizza and the train journey. Finally he was satisfied that he hadn't missed anything. She hadn't mentioned Danielle, but she thought she'd wait and see how things turned out before telling him about her.

'I love you, turtle,' her dad said finally.

Sunny smiled at the pet name he'd called her since she was a baby and used to peek out of her blanket looking, apparently, like a turtle peeping from its shell.

'I love you too,' Sunny said.

After she ended the call, a pang of homesickness made her stomach curl. She pictured her dad sitting at the dining table, looking at his reflection in the dark window to the garden, the *Game of Thrones* mug Aisha had bought him for his birthday full of green tea and steaming. The sound of the TV – always on too loud – bleeding through the wall.

As she opened the bathroom door the main door opened and banged into it and she heard someone swear in an Australian accent. Great, Danielle was back. Sunny had been half-hoping she would have found somewhere else to stay – she hadn't seemed that keen on sharing with three strangers – but no, she was back. Sunny stepped back into the bathroom and let Danielle walk into the main room.

'You're all in bed?!' Danielle said, incredulously.

'I'm not,' Sunny mumbled.

Danielle looked her up and down. 'But you're about to go to bed, right? They're not your usual clothes.'

Sunny was wearing black pyjama bottoms with white spots and a black long-sleeved T-shirt with built-in bra support.

'Yeah, I'm going to bed,' Sunny said.

'This is so not the party room,' Danielle said.

She kicked off her flip-flops and started wriggling out of her skinny jeans, telling them about how she'd been to Old Street to meet a guy she knew via Twitter. They'd bought pulled pork sandwiches from a street cart and been to an exhibition of graffiti art.

Sunny climbed the ladder to her top bunk and pulled Caspar out from his hiding place under her pillow. Could Danielle really be fourteen, like her? She didn't look much older, but the way she dressed and acted . . . And Sunny knew it wasn't a good idea to meet up with people you'd met on the internet. Certainly not on your own. And what even was graffiti art?

'Are you over here just for the summer?' she heard Kitty ask Danielle.

She felt like she should try to chat too – she would usually – but something about Danielle really rubbed her up the wrong way and she just couldn't face making conversation. She rolled on to her side and pulled the duvet up over her head.

Sunny couldn't sleep. She tried counting the cars going past on the street below. She tried to work out which were cars, which were taxis, which were buses, but that didn't help. She listened to people coming out of bars, laughing, shouting, the occasional shriek.

Her three roommates were all quiet. She didn't know for sure that they were asleep, but the room felt still and heavy, so she thought they probably were. It made her feel alone. She tucked Caspar into the space between her shoulder and jaw, where she'd sometimes carried him when she was little. Her dad used to joke that she was a pirate and Caspar was her ship's parrot, saying, 'Who's a pretty boy then?' in a silly voice to make Sunny laugh.

She thought about her dad in the lounge last week. Perched on the edge of the sofa and jiggling his legs, so she knew he was nervous. Or excited. One of the two. And then he'd told her that he was opening a practice with his brother, her uncle. In Richmond. And they were all moving.

He and Sunny's mum had found a house – he'd seen it in person, her mum had looked at it online – and Sunny and Hamzah would be going to the same school their cousins attended.

No discussion. A done deal.

9

Sunny was woken by her phone vibrating next to her ear. She'd put it under her pillow so she wouldn't miss it and then, at some point during a night of broken sleep, she'd moved it on top of her pillow, by her face.

The room was already light and she rolled on to her stomach and looked over towards the window. The blinds were down, but she could tell it was bright outside. She listened to the sounds of the Strand – trucks rumbling, a siren in the distance, shutters being raised on the shops. She didn't know how long it had taken her to get to sleep in the end, but it had felt like a long time. Long enough that the street had become almost quiet. Her head felt fuzzy and heavy and she had a crick in her neck.

'Anyone awake?' she heard Hannah say.

'I am,' she croaked.

There was a strangled groan from Kitty's bed. Nothing from Danielle.

'Are you going to pray?' Hannah asked her.

Sunny sat up slowly, her eyes still half closed. 'Yeah. Can I have the first shower?'

Hannah sat up too and nodded. Her hair was hanging over her face. She rubbed her eyes.

'Did you sleep okay?' Sunny asked.

'Yeah,' Hannah said. 'But it was a bit noisy.'

'Like now?' Sunny heard Danielle say from under the bed.

'Sorry,' Sunny said. 'But we have to get up anyway. For the course.'

Danielle groaned and the mattress creaked as she rolled over. 'Why'd I have to get a room with the goody-goodies.'

Sunny showered and got dressed in the bathroom, kicking herself for being so timid around Danielle. Danielle was rude and it was Sunny's room too – why did she feel like she had to tiptoe around her? She was always intimidated by the cool girls. Even Hannah when she first met her. Maybe she'd get to like Danielle in time. Although they only had two weeks.

Back in the bedroom, Hannah was out of bed in the T-shirt and shorts she'd slept in, rummaging through a pile of her clothes on the floor. Kitty was sitting on the desk chair in the far corner near the window, talking on the phone, presumably to Dylan. Danielle was still in bed.

Sunny's stomach flickered with anxiety, even though it wasn't her problem. In fact, it was nothing to do with her. If Danielle stayed in bed and missed the course, so what? It didn't make any difference to Sunny.

When Sunny got back from the prayer room, Hannah and Kitty were dressed, but Danielle didn't seem to have moved. Hannah pulled a face at Sunny.

Sunny just couldn't stand it.

'Danielle?' she said. 'Are you getting up?'

There was a groan from under the duvet.

'We're going to have breakfast now,' Sunny said. 'We're supposed to be leaving in half an hour.'

'Fine,' Danielle said, without moving.

'Okay,' Hannah said. 'See you later.'

And they left.

'I can't believe we have to share with someone,' Sunny said as they walked down the corridor to the kitchen.

Some of the other doors had been left open and

they could hear music coming from behind one of them.

'I never even thought about it,' Hannah said. 'Probably should've done, really. Should've known the rooms would be for four, not three.'

'Must be much harder for Danielle though,' Kitty said. 'We've just got one person we don't know – she's got the three of us.'

Sunny pulled a face. She knew Kitty was right – she'd really hate to be in Danielle's position, having to share with three strangers, but she didn't want to have to share with Danielle either.

'Is she just over for the summer?' Sunny asked Kitty. 'I heard you ask her, but I didn't hear her answer.'

'She didn't answer, actually,' Kitty said. 'So I don't know.'

The kitchen was busy and bright. Light slanted through the long windows, so bright that Sunny had to squint to see Steven, who was reading a paper and fiddling with his phone at the same time.

'Everyone okay?' Steven said.

He looked up, they all smiled and nodded, and he went back to his paper and phone.

The frightened-looking blond girl, Sophie, was

leaning against the counter eating a doughnut. She waved.

'There's doughnuts?' Hannah said.

'Just for today,' Steven said, smiling. 'Don't get used to it.'

'So are you taking us to class?' Kitty asked.

Steven nodded. 'Me and Liz. It's not far – just about five minutes' walk. We'll be leaving in about twenty minutes. Grab some breakfast.'

Sunny, Hannah and Kitty headed over to the counter and took a pastry and a glass of orange juice each. Joel was sitting at a table, his head resting on his arms. Other students straggled in, looking tired and dishevelled. A really short girl with bright blue hair came over and poured herself a glass of juice.

'Are you nervous?' she asked Kitty.

Kitty nodded.

'Good,' the girl said. 'Wait. I mean, it's not good that you're nervous, but it's good that I'm not the only one who is.'

'I knew what you meant,' Kitty said. 'I've never done anything like this before. Did you win a competition too?'

The girl nodded. 'There's four of us – me and

Miyuki –' she pointed at the Japanese girl who was in the corner on her phone – 'and Dillon and Joel. I'm Sarah.'

'I'm Kitty, this is Sunny and that's Hannah. We met Dillon and Joel yesterday.'

Hannah had sat down next to Joel who'd sat up and was looking at her blearily but cheerfully.

Sunny and Kitty sat down opposite, along with Sarah and Miyuki, who was still on her phone, but came over and joined them. And then Will arrived. He wasn't using his wheelchair – he had a stick. Sunny's first thought was that he looked taller and then she wanted to kick herself. She was so relieved she'd only thought it and it hadn't actually escaped from her mouth.

'Hey,' she said and took a bite of muffin so she wasn't tempted to say anything stupid.

Will grinned. 'The gang's all here!' And then he shook his head. 'Sorry. I say cheesy stuff when I'm nervous.'

'You're nervous?' Hannah said. 'You don't seem nervous.'

'You know how it's embarrassing when you have to walk into a room of people you don't know?' he said. 'Well imagine how much more embarrassing it is if you accidentally hit someone in the shin with your stick. Or if your wheelchair doesn't fit behind the desk and everyone has to wait while the room gets rearranged.' He grinned. 'The upside is, everyone always knows who I am.'

Will got a glass of juice and a doughnut, then they all sat down at the nearest empty table, Will hooking his stick on the edge.

'It sounds like it's going to be a good day,' Sunny said. 'At the studio, I mean.'

'Do you think?' Will said. 'I thought it looked a bit boring – introduction stuff. I'd rather get on with actually making a film.'

'Sunny loves the introduction stuff,' Hannah said. 'It appeals to her inner control freak.'

'Inner?' Kitty said, grinning.

'Shut up,' Sunny said. 'I just like to be organised. I like knowing what's going to happen. I like a plan.'

'Oh, you're one of those "organised fun" people,' Will said, grinning at her.

'I just feel better when I know what I'm doing,' Sunny said. 'I'm not, like, psycho about it or anything.'

'Hey!' The other chaperone, Liz, appeared at the end of the table, smiling brightly. 'How's everyone this morning?'

They all muttered about sleep and doughnuts and she nodded back at them.

'No chair today?' she asked Will, her eyebrows shooting up.

'Just for now,' Will said, lightly. 'I'll use the chair to get to the course.'

'Good, good,' Liz said. 'Now, I'd better grab one of those pastries before they all vanish!'

'She's obviously a morning person,' Hannah said, downing the last of her juice.

Will smiled. 'I get that kind of thing a lot. Health and safety. They want to make sure I'm not going to fall over and sue them.'

They sat in silence for a bit and then Will said, 'So aren't you going to ask what's wrong with me?' He grinned.

'I didn't know the right way to put it,' Sunny admitted. '"What's wrong?" seems, you know . . . wrong.'

'I've been asked worse,' Will said. 'I've got a thing called Hyper Mobility Syndrome, which very basically means that my joints move around too much. And they sometimes dislocate.'

The three girls winced.

'That sounds painful,' Kitty said.

Will smiled. 'Yeah. It is. Some days are worse than others. So when it's bad, I use the chair, other days – or if I'm not doing so much – I can manage without. But it causes exhaustion too, so I need to pace myself. So, you know, there'll be no clubbing for me.'

'Is everyone ready?' Steven called. 'We need to leave in about five minutes.'

'That's the cue for me to get my chair,' Will said.

Liz appeared at the end of the table again. 'I'll come with you,' she said.

'No,' Will said, unhooking his stick from the edge of the table and using it to push himself up from his seat. 'Thanks, but I can manage by myself.'

'Are you sure?' Liz said.

Sunny looked from Liz to Will and back again.

'I'm fine,' Will said. 'I promise.'

10

Sunny's phone buzzed in her pocket as they were waiting in the lobby for everyone else to make it down the stairs or, in Will's case, the lift.

'Your dad?' Kitty said as Sunny read the text.

Sunny nodded. 'Just wanted to wish me luck for our first day. And he says to say hello to you guys too.'

'He's so lovely,' Hannah said.

'Have you called your parents yet?' Sunny asked.

She realised she hadn't heard either of them talking to their families since they'd arrived.

'I called my mum last night,' Kitty said. 'She's been talking to Tom and telling him to come and keep an eye on us.' She rolled her eyes, but then she grinned.

'I left a message for mine,' Hannah said. 'Maybe she'll pick it up by the weekend . . .'

Sunny squeezed her friend's arm. She suspected that Hannah exaggerated her mum's disinterest, but it obviously still hurt her.

The lift doors opened and Will – using his wheelchair – joined them in the lobby.

'One of these days I'm going to wear a Superman suit under my clothes and come out of the lift transformed,' he said, grinning.

Sunny snorted with laughter and quickly covered her mouth with her hand. 'You totally should do that.'

He smiled at her and she felt her stomach flutter. She took a step backwards.

'Once,' Will said, 'I got in the lift with a bunch of other people – adults – and as it set off I said, "I know you're wondering why I asked you all here," but no one laughed or said anything. There was just an uncomfortable silence till I got out.'

'Ready?' Liz said, putting one hand on the back of Will's chair.

'Yep,' Will said and rolled himself towards the double doors.

'It's a straightforward walk,' Steven said from the door. 'So no one should get lost, but if you do –' he held up his mobile – 'call me and I'll come and find you. Don't panic!'

'He's gorgeous, isn't he?' Hannah said, as they set off down the Strand behind Will and Liz.

'Steven?' Sunny said. 'I didn't think he was your type.'

'You're very funny,' Hannah said. 'No. Will.'

'Yeah, he seems really nice,' Sunny said. 'His illness sounds horrible though.'

'I know,' Hannah said. 'Imagine having to deal with all that at our age.'

They turned off the Strand, and Sunny could see Covent Garden market up ahead. She'd walked this route on Google Maps. Every time she'd started to feel too nervous about the course, whenever she thought she might have to make some excuse and not go, she'd gone on Google Maps and wandered from the dorm to the school in a bunch of different directions, so it was funny to be there for real.

What you didn't get from Google Maps was the atmosphere. The sun was shining, the pavements were clean and Sunny felt excitement in the air. She almost wanted to break free from the group and run up to the market and look around. But she couldn't. And even if she could, she wouldn't. She didn't want to miss any of the course.

From Covent Garden they turned down a side street and Steven led them into a plain, grey-stone building with large tinted windows. They had to queue up to sign in and a short, young-looking boy ended up next to Sunny and introduced himself as Cameron. He didn't stop talking the whole time they were waiting to sign in – he'd done the course before and had a lot of thoughts on the subject. Sunny barely said a word, just nodded and occasionally said, 'Oh dear,' and tried not to make it obvious that she wanted to get away to be with her friends. When she turned round to look for them, she saw Kitty chatting to the girl with the blue hair and Hannah talking to Joel and twirling her hair. Sunny rolled her eyes.

Once they'd all signed in, they were directed to a room on the second floor. Cameron carried on talking all the way up the stairs. He'd already started making short films with his school's film club. He was really just taking the course again to 'perfect the craft'.

Upstairs the room was set out with desks just like school. There was something about it that made it seem better than school, Sunny thought, but she couldn't quite work out what it was. Maybe it was just that it was an old building with more character. The desks were wooden and at the front of the room there was an actual blackboard, rather than an interactive whiteboard. The ceilings sloped on either side and there were two large windows with views over the Covent Garden rooftops.

There was a bit of a backlog for actually getting inside the room and after a few seconds, Sunny realised it was because of Will.

'You okay?' she said, squeezing past a couple of the other students to stand next to him.

'Could you give me a hand?' Will gestured at the handles on his wheelchair.

'Oh yeah,' Sunny said. 'Course. Sorry.'

She steered him over to the desk he pointed out. At the back, next to the window, there was a sort of alcove, so it had more room around it than the other desks.

He thanked her and pulled out the chair next to him, motioning for her to sit down. Sunny looked back at Cameron, who was still standing near the door and now talking to the girl with the blue hair. Sunny felt a pang of guilt for escaping him, but not enough to go back.

'Thank you,' she said to Will.

Will grinned. 'No worries. You looked like you needed rescuing.'

Sunny raised one eyebrow. 'I did not need rescuing. He's nice! He just –'

'Doesn't stop talking. I know. And I didn't mean to suggest you couldn't have, you know, saved yourself.'

Sunny rolled her eyes. 'You're my knight in shining armour?'

'No armour, sorry,' he said. 'Unless the chair counts? But it could do with a polish. Not sure knights are meant to have quite so many crisps crushed in their armour.'

'Oh, I bet they did,' Sunny said. 'Ye Olde Crispes.'

'Pringles of Yore.'

Sunny was trying to think of another crisp joke when she noticed the chatter that had previously filled the room had died down. She saw that the teacher had arrived and she also spotted Kitty and Hannah who were sitting together on the opposite side of the room. They waved and Hannah widened her eyes, which Sunny knew was about her sitting with Will.

The teacher waited until everyone was completely silent and then introduced himself as Mr Berman. He was American, looked quite old, and was wearing a very wrinkled shirt and baggy cords. He told them he was there to teach them about the history of film and, for the next hour and a half, he showed them clips from old movies on a screen he pulled down from the ceiling, explaining why they were classics.

It was really fascinating to see the progression from the early silent black-and-white films to something technically cutting edge like *Avatar*.

'That was brilliant,' Sunny said as she wheeled Will out to the hallway where everyone was queuing up in front of a vending machine.

'I've hardly seen any of those films,' Will said. 'I need to do some swotting up.'

'Me too,' Sunny said.

Will looked back over his shoulder at Sunny. 'You know you don't need to push me, right?'

Sunny blushed. 'Sorry, I forgot.'

He grinned. 'It's okay. It's nice that you want to help.'

Sunny remembered Will telling Liz he didn't need any help at breakfast and wondered what that was about. Maybe he didn't want special treatment from the staff? She could understand that.

By the end of the day, Sunny felt like they'd had a really good introduction to the history of film and film techniques. Even Mr Berman had turned out not to be as dry as he first appeared – singing along with the excerpts from the musicals and making them laugh with impersonations. Sunny couldn't wait for the rest of the course.

11

'I hate to admit it,' Hannah said, pouring herself a glass of orange juice and sitting down at one of the long tables. 'But you were right.'

The previous evening they'd all been so exhausted from the first day of classes that Sunny had convinced them to stay in and have an early night. It hadn't ended up being all that early because the other students didn't quieten down until gone eleven, but Sunny had actually managed to fall asleep pretty quickly after that.

'I'm always right,' Sunny said, grinning.

Hannah snorted. 'But that means we have to go out tonight.'

'I thought we could walk up to Piccadilly Circus,' Kitty said. 'It's not far and I really want to see it.'

'And we can get something to eat up there too,' Hannah agreed.

'We'll see,' Sunny said. 'We might be too tired again.'

'I don't care how tired I am,' Hannah said. 'I refuse to spend every night in our room, waiting to see if Danielle comes back.'

After not turning up to classes at all the previous day, Danielle had returned to their room just before curfew and then spent ages in the bathroom. She'd got up that morning when Sunny's alarm went off, but was still in the shower when they'd left for breakfast. She still hadn't appeared when it was time to leave for class, so they headed to Covent Garden with Will again and the four of them sat together.

Today's teacher was called Juliet and she had dyed black hair down to her waist, thick black-rimmed glasses and a squeaky voice. She had them write a short scene, using only dialogue, and then read it out to each other.

Sunny wrote a version of saying goodbye to her parents at the station – really hamming up her dad's requests for her to keep in touch and her mum's worry about having left the car illegally parked. In her version, she was totally chilled and just keen to get off to London, though the truth was she'd been horribly nervous.

Sunny was embarrassed reading hers aloud, but Will laughed in all the right places.

'That's really good,' he said. 'You should maybe work it up to something else.'

'I don't know about that,' Sunny said. 'It was just the first thing that popped into my head.'

'Something to think about though,' Will said.

Will's script was really good too. He'd written a conversation between superheroes who were trying to do everyday stuff and he didn't just read like she had, he properly acted it. Sunny laughed so much she had to go and get a drink of water.

Then Juliet had them write the same scene but using description and no dialogue. Sunny found that her scene felt completely different – sad and sort of melancholy. It made her miss her parents and feel slightly guilty for mocking them, however affectionately, in the previous version.

Steven had told Will about a café nearby, so Sunny, Hannah and Kitty went along there with him. It was a tiny place that didn't even look like a café from the outside. It was more like a door to someone's house – it even had a gate. Inside it was small, just one room with six wooden tables. The waitress came to the door as soon as she saw Will and moved chairs out of the way so he could wheel himself up to a table. The walls were covered with framed theatre programmes and a theatre soundtrack was playing, although Sunny wasn't sure what show it was from.

By the time they'd all sat down, the waitress was back with a jug of water and glasses and the menus. As well as sandwiches, they had stuff like beans on toast, cheese on toast and school-dinner-type stuff for pudding.

The four of them ordered sandwiches and talked about the morning's class while they waited.

'I wasn't looking forward to the screenwriting,' Hannah said, 'but I loved it.'

'Me too,' Sunny said.

'You were brilliant at it,' Will said to Sunny. 'I loved your dialogue version.'

Sunny smiled at him. 'It was really interesting how different the two versions felt. It made me think about how the way you tell a story is important. As important as the actual story, I mean. I'm glad she didn't make us read it out to the class though. Will properly acted his one.'

Will grinned. 'Well I want to be an actor so it'd be a bit crap if I couldn't read in front of people.'

'Why are you doing the film-making course if you want to be an actor?' Hannah asked him.

Will shrugged. 'I figured it couldn't hurt. I think people need to be able to do more than one thing these days. And particularly with this –' he gestured at his chair – 'the more stuff I can do the better. And I thought it'd be a laugh.'

'I don't understand you people who know what you want to do,' Hannah said. 'We're only fourteen!'

'You don't know?' Will said, pretending to be outraged.

'I haven't a clue!' Hannah said.

'I bet you have a bit,' Kitty said. 'What would your dream job be?'

Hannah frowned then shook her head. 'Nope. I don't know. Honest.'

'You like singing,' Sunny said.

'I do, yeah. But I'm not good enough to be an actual singer.'

'Do you know what you want to do?' Will asked Sunny.

'Sort of,' she said, pouring herself more water. 'I know what I am going to do anyway.'

'What's that?' Will said.

'I'm going to university to study medicine.'

'You want to be a doctor?'

Sunny shook her head. 'Not really. I mean, I don't

not want to do it. I think it'll be good and I hope I'll be good at it . . .'

'But?' Will said.

'But my dad's a doctor.' Sunny said. 'A GP. And I know it would mean a lot to him for me to do the same.'

Will gave her a sad smile. 'That's no good though. It's your life.'

Sunny laughed. 'Yeah. Sometimes.'

'What would they say if you said no?' Kitty asked.

Sunny shook her head. 'I don't know. It's just not really an option. I couldn't disappoint them like that.'

'I always though it was a stereotype,' Will said. 'The Asian doctor thing.'

Sunny smiled. 'It is. But that doesn't mean it's not true sometimes.'

'Your dad is so lovely though,' Kitty said. 'I'm sure he'd understand if you wanted to do something different.'

'I know,' Sunny said. 'But he's very traditional in a lot of ways. And he wants me to have a secure job and money, you know? And this is his way of making sure I'll be okay.'

'But what if you wanted to do something else

secure with money?' Hannah said. 'Like a lawyer? My mum's a lawyer,' she told Will.

'I don't know,' Sunny said. 'I think he'd understand that more. I think he'd be disappointed, but it wouldn't be a catastrophe. If I went home and said I wanted to be an actor, that would be a catastrophe.'

Hannah frowned. 'It's your life though.'

Sunny smiled. 'Not yet it's not.'

12

After classes were over everyone headed back to the dorm. Steven was allowing them to make their own way back, so they walked diagonally across the piazza, stopped to watch a magician performing in front of the church and then had a bit of a wander through the market.

Sunny thought about the market at home – how it smelled of raw meat and how the stallholders shouted, 'All right, love?' at Hannah and Kitty, but never at her. Here, the stalls sold vintage jewellery and artisan beers and the air smelled of soapy perfume and no one shouted anything at any of them.

She wondered whether Richmond had a market. If it did, her cousins had never taken her there. She assumed it would be more like this one than the one at home and while she was no fan of the market there at all, she thought she might almost miss it.

'You fancy Will,' Hannah said in a sing-song voice, once they were back in their room.

Sunny had been to pray and they were getting ready to go out. Danielle was nowhere to be seen.

'I don't,' Sunny said automatically.

'He fancies you then,' Hannah said.

'Oh you always think everyone fancies everyone,' Sunny said, switching her phone on.

'I knew Sam fancied you, didn't I?' Hannah said.

Both Sunny and Kitty said, 'Ha!' at the same time.

'You thought he fancied Kitty!' Sunny said.

'Well, I knew he fancied someone,' Hannah said, grinning. 'I just got the signals a bit crossed.'

Hannah pulled her top off and headed for the bathroom.

'So you definitely don't fancy Will?' she said as she passed Sunny's bed. 'He's so cute!'

Sunny's phone vibrated in her hand. She had three messages – one from her dad, two from Sam.

'No,' she said. 'I don't fancy him. He's lovely, but . . .'

'Is it cos of the wheelchair?' Hannah called through the open bathroom door.

'No, it's not cos of the wheelchair! And are you on the loo? I'm not talking to you if you're on the loo.'

'Nuh!' Hannah shouted back. 'Am creaning ma teef!'

'Oh. Okay.' Sunny put her phone in the pocket of her bag and took out the clothes she was planning to wear. 'I just don't fancy him.'

She heard Hannah spit and then say, 'But why wouldn't you? What's not to fancy?'

Sunny shook her head. 'So you fancy him, do you?'

Hannah reappeared. 'I would, but tragically for Will, I am spoken for. Currently. Of course, this may change. I haven't decided yet.' She grinned.

Sunny laughed. 'I'm sure he'll be crying himself to sleep every night. Is there an iron in here?'

'What do *you* think?' Hannah stepped into her skirt. 'But I mean, if he is interested, don't you think you could . . . you know?'

'No,' Sunny said, opening the wardrobe to check for an iron. Hannah was right – there wasn't one. 'I don't know.'

'Well you're not allowed to go out with boys at home, right? But you're not at home.'

'No, I'm not allowed to go out with boys at all, not just at home.' Sunny took a coat hanger out of the wardrobe and hung her tunic top on it.

'But if your parents don't know . . .' Hannah said.

Sunny shook her head. 'I wouldn't do that to them. They trusted me enough to let me come here. Why would I break that trust?'

'God,' Hannah said. 'How are we even friends?'

'I have no idea,' Sunny said, grinning. 'I'm going for a shower.'

She took her holdall with her into the bathroom and as soon as she'd locked the door and hung her top up, hoping the steam from the shower would 'iron' it, she sat down on the loo with her phone.

Her dad's message said: *Hope you're having fun, turtle. And working hard. We miss you xx*

It made her miss him too. So much that she almost wanted to hug the phone, but that would be weird. She smiled at it though, while she replied that, yes, she was working hard, but having fun and missing them too. And that London was sunny and noisy and Covent Garden was cool.

There were also two messages from Sam.

The first said: *Have you seen the changing of the guards?*

Frowning, Sunny was about to reply when she realised she should probably read his second message first. She was right.

It said: *Dunno why they don't do it somewhere private.*

Sunny giggled, even thought the joke was dumb.

Saw it today, she texted. *One of them changed into Superman and flew off.*

As she was getting ready, she remembered Will's joke about Superman and laughed out loud. He was funny. She liked him. But she didn't fancy him, did she? She wasn't sure.

Danielle had made it to class after lunch, but had disappeared while they were in the market and she wasn't back by the time the three of them were ready to go out.

'Should we tell someone, do you think?' Kitty said, tying the laces on her Converse.

Hannah shook her head. 'Nah. Not unless they ask. It's none of our business, is it.'

'But maybe she's in trouble?' Kitty said.

'If she doesn't come back tonight, we'll tell someone,' Hannah said. 'But if she's off with a boyfriend or something she's not going to be impressed if we snitch.'

'Snitch?' Kitty laughed. 'We're not in prison.'

'You know what I mean,' Hannah said. 'Maybe she's sharing with someone else. Is her stuff still here?'

There was nothing on the bed, but when Sunny looked, Danielle's expensive-looking holdall was still underneath, along with a couple of pairs of knickers – Sunny really hoped they were clean.

'I'm sure she can look after herself,' Hannah said. 'She's probably off with someone else from Twitter.'

'It just seems weird that she hardly comes to class and we never know where she is,' Kitty said. 'We should probably say something.'

'Okay,' Hannah said. 'Tomorrow. We'll tell someone tomorrow.'

13

At Piccadilly Circus, Kitty took photos of them on the Eros steps and then made Sunny and Hannah pose so the light from the billboards shone on their faces.

They went to M&M World and had their photos taken with giant M&Ms and then got a rickshaw up Regent Street so Hannah could go to Top Shop. Once they'd dragged her out of there, they ordered pasta in a café off Carnaby Street.

Sunny left her phone on the table while she went to the salad bar and when she got back Kitty and Hannah were grinning at her.

'What?'

Hannah pointed at Sunny's phone. 'You got a text. From Sam.'

'Why are you reading my texts?' Sunny said, sitting down and putting her phone back in her pocket.

'We didn't,' Kitty said. 'It just popped up with his name.'

'Aren't you going to read it?' Hannah said.

Sunny shoved some garlic bread in her mouth and shook her head. 'I'll read it later.'

'When you're alone?' Hannah said, grinning.

Sunny rolled her eyes. 'When I'm away from you two, anyway. If I *can* ever get away from you two!'

Hannah laughed. 'As if you could quit us.'

'Is that why you're not interested in Will?' Kitty said. 'Cos of Sam?'

Sunny shook her head. 'There is nothing going on with Sam!'

'But he likes you,' Hannah said. 'Do you just not fancy him?'

'It's not about whether I fancy him or not,' Sunny said. 'I can't have a boyfriend.'

'I don't understand it,' Hannah said. 'I know your parents are religious and everything, but I don't see why you're not allowed a boyfriend. I mean, they know that everyone your age has boyfriends, right?'

'Not everyone,' Kitty said.

'Or girlfriends, yeah,' Hannah said. 'You know what I mean, though? It'll be weird if you don't. Don't they care about that?'

Sunny shook her head. 'They wouldn't even think

about it. They don't care if people think I'm weird. They'd rather people thought that than thought I wasn't respecting myself or something. You know? I mean, people already think I'm weird cos of the hijab, so . . .' She shrugged.

'It just seems mad,' Hannah said. 'They have to let you be a teenager!'

'I am being a teenager,' Sunny said. 'Just a teenager who doesn't happen to have a boyfriend. I don't think that's so freakish really.'

'But doesn't it bother you?' Hannah said.

She reached over and nicked a cherry tomato from the edge of Sunny's plate where she'd lined them up. Hannah always ate Sunny's tomatoes.

'Not having a boyfriend?' Sunny said. 'No.'

'But what about Sam?' Hannah said. 'You like him –'

'He's my friend,' Sunny said. 'And that's fine.'

'Does he know he's just your friend?' Hannah said.

Sunny nodded. 'Yes. I told him.'

She'd told him because he'd asked her out. He'd actually waited for her after school and asked if he could walk her home. They'd walked up through the park and along Vicky Road and were almost at the end of Sunny's road before he asked and then it had come out in one long word, 'Doyouwantogotothecinemawithmesometime?'

He looked so cute – he'd been messing with his hair all the way from school so it was sticking up in tufts and his cheeks were pink with embarrassment – that Sunny almost wished she could have said yes.

But instead she said no and told him why not. He said he understood, but Sunny wasn't sure he did and was worried about how he'd be at school the next day. Luckily he'd acted as if nothing had happened and carried on just being the mate she had a laugh with in French and who sometimes wolf-whistled at her in the park to wind her up.

But when he'd found out she was going to London, he'd asked for her mobile number and she hadn't been able to think of a good reason not to give it to him and now he was sending texts and she wasn't sure why. Or what she should do about it.

But she definitely wasn't interested in him.

'What about you, anyway?' Sunny asked Hannah. 'Have you spoken to Louis yet?'

'I'm going to FaceTime him tonight,' she said. 'When we get back. See if absence really does make the heart fonder.'

'And if it doesn't?' Sunny said.

'Then that Joel's pretty cute, don't you think?' Hannah grinned.

When they got back to their room, the bathroom door was shut and they could hear the shower running. Danielle's clothes – jeans, top, bra and knickers – were on the floor next to her bed.

'I don't understand her,' Sunny said, walking so far around the clothes that she almost bumped into the opposite wall. 'Why would you leave them there like that?'

'She wants us to know she doesn't care what we think,' Hannah said. 'It's attention seeking. Just ignore her.'

Sunny yanked her holdall out of the wardrobe and put it on the table under the window, sorting her night things to the top and checking the zip-pull plastic bag with her laundry in was easily accessible. When there was no sign of Danielle coming out of the bathroom – the water was still running – she cleaned her face with a baby wipe, surprised to find it was really dirty.

'My face is rotten!' she said, chucking the wipe in the bin under the table.

'I noticed that when I took my make-up off last night,' Hannah said from her top bunk. She was already in her pyjamas. Sunny hadn't even noticed her change. 'Must be cos of the pollution.'

'When Tom first moved down he told me he had black bogies,' Kitty said. 'When he picked his nose.'

'Brothers are horrible,' Sunny said. 'Actually I need to buy a postcard tomorrow to send to Hamzah. He wants one shaped like a London bus.'

'I'll get one for Grace too,' Kitty said. 'She said she's going to send me one, but I doubt she will.'

'I'll send my mum one,' Hannah said. 'I'll put "Remember me?" on the back.'

Hannah was already lying on her bed, ready to FaceTime with Louis, and Sunny could see Kitty was about to ring Dylan so, even though she was still dressed, she climbed up to her bunk. Could she get changed up there? If she had to. She really didn't want to. And surely Danielle couldn't be in the bathroom much longer, could she?

By the time Sunny had read a chapter of *Great Expectations*, the first book on next year's reading list, the shower had stopped running, but Danielle still didn't come out.

'Should we check on her?' Sunny said, but Kitty

and Hannah were both chatting and didn't reply.

Maybe Danielle was dead in the bottom of the shower, Sunny thought. But then the water wouldn't have stopped, would it? She was probably shaving her legs or plucking her eyebrows or something.

Sunny rolled on to her front and took out her phone. She hadn't checked it for a while and she hadn't rung her dad either. She called and got his voicemail, so she left a message telling him she'd ring him tomorrow. Then she rang again, just to listen to his voice on the message.

He was probably doing something to the house – repainting the render or cleaning out the guttering or something. One of the jobs he'd been talking about forever, but would now be getting on with because they were going to sell the house.

Her parents had always been the kind of people who liked to get things done. Her mum because she always wanted to be organised – she couldn't stand any sort of disorder or mess – and her dad because he always got really excited about change. Sunny couldn't understand that at all. It wasn't normal to love change, was it? How did that work, when you had a life you loved and were used to? When you knew your way around and had friends you could trust? How could anyone say, 'Oh we'll just chuck this all in and go and have an adventure'?

And, yes, she would know people in Richmond. She loved her family there – her cousin Amirah was one of her favourite people in the world and they always had a great time when they visited.

But visiting wasn't the same as moving. And Sunny really didn't want to move.

14

'I can't believe she's just not going to come to the classes,' Sunny said as she, Hannah, Kitty and Will made their way to college the next morning.

It was another clear and warm day, but Danielle had, once again, just stayed in bed through all her roommates' alarms and preparations. The previous night, Sunny had been asleep before Danielle had even come out of the bathroom. She hadn't apologised or anything, she'd just got into her bed and started messing about on her phone.

'Can we report her to someone?' Sunny asked. 'I mean, we could ask for her to be moved to a different room maybe?'

'I don't know,' Hannah said. 'I think that's probably not a good idea. It'll make us look petty, you know?'

'But I couldn't even use the bathroom last night – we could complain about that, couldn't we?' Sunny said.

'Hannah's right, I think,' Kitty said. 'We should probably try to talk to her before we talk to anyone else.'

'Ugh,' Sunny said. 'Can you do it while I'm praying or something?'

'Are you scared of her?' Hannah said, grinning.

'Yes,' Sunny said.

Hannah bumped her with her arm. 'Don't be scared. You've got me and Kitty.'

Sunny snorted. 'I'm not scared of her, she just . . .' Sunny frowned, trying to think of how to describe it.

'She's a bit much,' Kitty said.

'Yeah,' Sunny said.

'People say that about me though,' Hannah said. 'I think *you've* even said it before now.'

Sunny smiled at her friend. 'But you're nice. She's not nice. I don't trust her.'

'Maybe she's just insecure,' Will said.

Hannah booed and he laughed. 'I know. But maybe she was nervous and she decided to pretend to be confident and she went too far. You know?'

'Maybe,' Sunny said. 'Or maybe she's just really obnoxious.'

Will laughed. 'Maybe. But you probably do need to talk to her to find out.'

'Does anyone know what a vox pop is?' the teacher, Jax – a tall skinny guy with a bald head and a pierced eyebrow – said. He was perched on the edge of the desk and sat, staring at them, smiling in anticipation. But no one answered.

'Right,' he said, nodding. 'It's when you go out and get opinions from people on the street. You'll have seen it on the news – random people saying they don't agree with a proposed new supermarket or something like that. Yeah? So that's what we're going to do today.'

He stood up and walked round to the back of the desk. 'You're going to form teams – you can pick your own, I'm not going to put you together – then decide between you who's in charge of the cameras, sound, questions and editing. And then we're going to go out and talk to people.'

Sunny, Hannah, Kitty and Will were already sitting together, so they immediately started trying to decide who was going to do what. Will had just volunteered to edit when the door to the classroom opened and the teacher said, 'Ah-ha! A late arrival. Who has space in their group?'

'Yeah, sorry,' a voice said. A voice Sunny knew all too well.

Sunny was scared to look up. She didn't want

Danielle in their group, but inevitably Danielle made her way across the room, knocking a couple of bags off the backs of chairs on the way, and sat down at the end of the row next to Kitty.

'Hey,' she said. 'I finally made it!'

'Yeah,' Sunny said. 'Great.'

'High-five her,' Hannah whispered in Sunny's ear. 'In the face.'

Down on the street, Jax suggested they go in different directions, so as not to be targeting the same people.

'How about that park we went to?' Sunny said.

'Sounds good to me,' Will said.

'Sorry about last night,' Danielle said as they waited for the traffic lights to change.

Sunny looked at Kitty and Hannah.

'I don't sleep very well,' Danielle said. 'Takes me ages to drop off, so I've got this big routine I have to go through? It's a pain, honestly.'

'I didn't even get to use the bathroom,' Sunny said.

And Hannah was right, it did sound petty – she was glad she hadn't gone to see Steven about it.

'Yeah, sorry,' Danielle said. 'I'll wait for you all to go to bed in future.'

They crossed the road and it was only as they headed

down the narrow street that Sunny remembered the builders and their catcalling. She really hoped they weren't still there. Danielle was wearing tiny loose shorts that actually showed a bit of her bum cheeks, gold sandals that buckled almost up to her knees, a tiny top and huge sunglasses on top of her head. They hadn't even got halfway down the road before Sunny heard them. Whistling. Shouting. Barking.

Danielle lit up like she was at a club. She actually waved at them and her walk became even more wiggly than usual.

Sunny could feel her face burning. She'd literally only just started thinking Danielle might be okay. As soon as they were past the workmen and in the park, she said, 'What did you do that for?!'

'What?' Danielle said, taking her sunglasses off her head and putting them on her face.

'Why would you encourage them?'

Danielle laughed. 'Oh, it's just a bit of fun.'

'It is not!' Sunny said. 'It's dangerous and offensive.'

'For you, maybe,' Danielle said.

Even from behind the sunglasses, Sunny could tell Danielle was looking her up and down. All the anger went out of her in one burst and suddenly she felt miserable and slightly ashamed.

'So what am I doing?' Danielle said, clearly deciding that the conversation with Sunny was over. 'I thought I could do the interviewing? I've done it before and I'm pretty good at it.'

'I think we should take it in turns,' Hannah said. 'So we all get to try everything.'

'Good idea,' Will said. He had the laptop in its bag on his actual lap. He opened it up and Kitty took out the camera from its bag hanging on the back of Will's chair.

Danielle decided she would find the people to interview, but rather than approaching everyone who came into the park, she dismissed almost everyone as 'too boring', 'too old', 'too foreign'. She kept changing the questions the rest of them wanted to ask and actually exchanged mobile numbers with a student from Argentina.

'He's not "too foreign" apparently,' Hannah said as they watched Danielle flick her hair and touch the student's arm.

'We're actually getting some pretty good film,' Will said. 'She's good at getting people to talk.'

The student left, turning back for a few last looks at Danielle, and then Sunny took the opportunity to tell her to take a break.

'Hannah's going to have a turn at asking the questions for a bit, okay? And I'm going to take the camera. Do you want the laptop?'

Danielle shrugged. 'I just want to sit for a bit, you know? I'm knackered.'

She sat down on a bench, stretched her long legs out in front and tipped her face up to the sun.

They spent the next hour or so stopping everyone who was willing to stop. Some people said, 'Sorry, no time,' as they rushed past. Some people totally blanked them, acting as if they weren't even there. Some people talked for so long that Sunny pretended there was a problem with the camera so they'd go and they could speak to someone else. And some lanky teenage boys shouted, 'Get a job,' at them from the top of an open-top bus.

But Sunny found she loved every minute of it. She loved watching the interviews through the camera, zooming in on people's faces or out to show more of the park. Whenever they were waiting for someone to talk to, Sunny filmed whatever was nearby and frequently had to be pulled away from whatever it was because she'd become engrossed. She actually missed one person altogether because she'd zoomed in on a bee inside a flower and couldn't stop filming until it had flown away.

By the time they had to go back and meet Steven, they all felt like they had enough film to work with.

'That was fun,' Sunny said as they walked back up the narrow street. She was relieved to see that the builders had gone.

'Hey,' Sunny said. 'Where's Danielle?'

'Oh crap,' Hannah said. 'When did she leave?'

'I didn't even notice!' Sunny said. 'We should probably go back. In case she's still in the park somewhere.'

'I bet she went off with that guy,' Hannah said.

'She might've just gone to the loo or something though,' Kitty said. 'We'd better go back and see if she's around.'

'I'll come with you,' Hannah said to Kitty. 'You go back with Will, Sunny.' From behind Will's back, she gave Sunny an elaborate wink.

Sunny shook her head. 'It's fine, I'll –'

'Come on, Kits,' Hannah said, grabbing Kitty's arm. 'We're going on a Danielle hunt!'

Sunny sighed. There was no arguing with Hannah once she'd made her mind up about something.

'So,' Will said once they'd gone. 'Awkward.' He grinned.

Sunny's breath caught in her chest.

'I've got a boyfriend,' she blurted out.

Will's eyebrows shot up. 'Oh! Oh, okay. I didn't realise.'

Sunny felt like she wanted to be sick. 'Sorry, I don't know why I said that. It's not like you –'

'No, it's okay. I mean, I like you. I didn't know you had a boyfriend. But that's cool.'

'Yeah. Um. He's at home. Obviously. His name's Sam.' She couldn't stop talking. Why couldn't she stop talking?

'That's who's been texting?' Will said. 'I've seen you checking your phone.'

Sunny nodded. She hadn't even realised she'd been checking it, but she certainly wasn't going to tell Will she'd mostly been texting with her dad. 'Yeah. He texts me. A lot.'

She sounded like an idiot. And it wasn't even true.

Will smiled. 'That's great. You must be missing him.'

Sunny nodded. 'We'd better set off,' she said. She really didn't want them to still be standing there discussing her imaginary boyfriend when Hannah and Kitty got back.

15

On the street outside the dorm, Tom hugged Kitty, rocking her from side to side, while she laughed and tried to wriggle free. He hugged Hannah too and then sort of awkwardly held his arms out to Sunny, as if he didn't know whether it was okay to hug her or not. She half grabbed his arms and did a sort of half hug, but they were both embarrassed and she was annoyed with herself that she hadn't thought of some way of avoiding it. The embarrassment, not the hug.

'It's so great to see you all!' Tom said.

He looked really good. His hair was a bit longer than the last time Sunny had seen him – at the awards presentation for the film-making competition they'd won – and she could understand why Hannah had had such a crush on him when they were younger.

Tom looked around, as if he was trying to remember

which way to go, and then headed back along the Strand.

'So how's it going so far?' he asked them. 'What did you do today?'

As they walked, Kitty told him about the course, while Hannah chimed in with some extra details. They told him about losing Danielle in the park the previous day and how she'd been back at the dorm when they'd got there, getting ready to go out with a boy she'd just met.

'Steam came out of Sunny's ears,' Hannah said. 'It was hilarious.'

'You don't like her?' Tom asked Sunny.

She shook her head. 'I don't even know why exactly, she just . . .' She tried to think of the right words, but couldn't find them.

'Rubs you up the wrong way?' Tom suggested. 'That happens. Especially when you're spending so much time with someone.'

'It was better today,' Sunny said. 'She was late for class and we'd already started what we were doing, so she was put with another group.'

They'd spent the day working on a script for a TV show and, after reading a few scripts, they'd actually been allowed to go off and watch their favourite TV shows for research. They'd learned that often that's how TV writers get started – writing a 'spec script' for an already established show. Sunny's head had been buzzing with ideas for her own shows all day.

They'd ended up writing a *Doctor Who* episode, since it was the only show the four of them could agree on, but it had been fun. Sunny had loved writing the dialogue and then reading it out with Will, particularly since he was a huge Whovian and added lots of detail Sunny wouldn't have thought of.

As the four of them – Sunny, Hannah, Kitty and Tom – walked along the Strand, Sunny found herself looking around London rather than talking. There was just so much to see. Even ordinary things – a branch of H&M, black cabs – were exciting because they were in London. But she also found herself writing stories in her head – what if the man she saw waving for a black cab was on his way to a first date with the woman of his dreams? What if she stood him up? What if the cab crashed on the way there and she thought she'd been stood up? She thought about the *Doctor Who* script they'd written and wondered about cab-driver aliens or the tube as a portal to another world.

'She's miles away,' Sunny heard Kitty say.

'What?' Sunny said. 'Sorry.'

The other three were grinning at her.

'I was just thinking about the script,' she said.

'Tom was just asking if you're enjoying the course,' Kitty said.

'I think that's a "yes" then?' Tom said, smiling.

Sunny nodded. 'I'm loving it. But I'm seeing stories everywhere.'

As they walked towards Covent Garden, they pointed out to Tom where the course took place.

'Oh yeah,' he said. 'Jack's done some stuff there. A music for film class, I think.'

'Did he enjoy it?' Hannah asked.

'Yeah, he said it was great,' Tom said. 'Though he was teaching there, not learning.'

'Oh, sorry!' Hannah said and she actually blushed. 'I forgot he worked in films.'

Sunny looked at Kitty and grinned. Obviously Hannah's crush hadn't totally gone away.

'How is he?' Kitty asked.

Tom grinned. 'He's doing great, thanks.'

'What does he do exactly?' Sunny asked.

'Music videos mainly,' Tom said. 'He likes the challenge of making films that go with the song without being really obvious, you know?'

'We've got to produce a short film at the end of the course,' Sunny said.

'You should definitely talk to him then,' Tom said. 'He'll give you some tips. Do you know what you're going to do yet?'

Sunny shook her head. 'We're waiting for inspiration. All we've got so far is that the theme is "conflict".'

Tom laughed. 'That's a pretty wide brief.'

'Right?' Kitty said. 'And we need to learn how to actually do most of it first. We're learning loads though. It's full-on.'

'I'll talk to Jack,' Tom said. 'See when he's free. Sooner would be better then?'

Sunny nodded. 'I think so. And if he hasn't got time to meet up, maybe we could ring him or talk on Skype?'

Tom nodded. 'No problem. I'll let you know. Talking of Skype . . . how's Dylan?'

Kitty's cheeks went pink. 'She's really good.'

They walked up a busy, pedestrianised street. A guy was playing a steel drum outside the station. Tom yelped with laughter and Sunny joined in when she recognised the song. It was 'Kiss the Girl' from *The Little Mermaid*.

'Very funny,' Kitty said, pretending to be annoyed.

'Listen, it was hard work arranging that!' Tom joked.

Kitty bumped him with her arm.

'So everything's okay now?' Tom asked her. 'School and everything?'

'It's better than it was,' Kitty said. 'I still get stupid comments sometimes, but it's not as bad as I thought it was going to be.'

'I told you it would be okay,' Tom said, bumping her back.

They turned left at the station and walked down a curved road that made Sunny want to stop and take everything in. The sun turned the buildings white and the windows gold. The contrast with the bright blue sky above made Sunny wish she had the course camera with her. Maybe she could make a film about London rooftops. She'd heard people say you should look up in New York, but London was pretty gorgeous above street level too.

'Here we are,' Tom said, stopping outside a restaurant with dark windows decorated with gold writing.

Inside it was bright and cool with plain tables and bare brick walls, not unlike the café they'd been to for lunch earlier in the week. But much bigger and much busier.

'I've reserved a booth,' Tom told the woman who came to greet them.

They followed her through the restaurant. Sunny couldn't keep up with all the stuff to look at, from the other customers to the pictures on the walls to a huge jewel-coloured glass chandelier in the centre of the ceiling. The room was buzzing and Sunny felt like she was buzzing just by being there.

The booth was just what Sunny wanted it to be. Red and padded with a Formica table in the middle – like something from an American diner. Kitty sat next to her brother, so Sunny slid in next to Hannah.

They ordered some drinks and then Tom asked Kitty how their mum was doing and while they talked, Sunny looked around the room.

'Are you okay?' Hannah asked her.

'Yes,' Sunny said. 'Why?'

'You look a bit like this?' Hannah pulled a dopey, dazzled-looking face.

Sunny laughed. 'I didn't expect to like it this much.'

'The restaurant?' Hannah asked.

'London.'

She realised she was picking at the skin around her

thumbnail and moved her hands under the table.

'Do you ever think about living here?' she asked Hannah.

Hannah shrugged. 'Not really. I'm not you – I don't think that far ahead. I wouldn't rule it out though.'

'Me and Dylan want to move here,' Kitty said, breaking off from talking to her brother. 'It was one of the first things we talked about. She wants to go to college in London.'

'I think it would be cool,' Sunny said. 'But I don't know . . . I think it would feel too big. If you lived here, I mean. You know, at home we know everyone. You couldn't do that here. I think it might be a bit lonely.'

'I worried about that when I first came here,' Tom said, smiling at Sunny. 'I think it's easy to be overwhelmed by London. You have to make an effort to get out and meet people, make friends. When I first moved here I hated it. I was always thinking about going home. Got as far as Euston once . . .'

'I didn't know that!' Kitty said. 'I thought you always loved it.'

'No, not always,' Tom said. 'It's just easy to get homesick, I think. Especially when you can't afford to go home much.'

Sunny did worry about that. About how often she'd actually get a chance to go home and see Kitty and Hannah. Wasn't it much more likely that they'd lose touch? They'd promise to always be friends and everything, she knew they would, but it was much harder to be friends with a couple of hundred miles between you. The thought of it made her want to cry.

16

'Maybe I should do the voiceover?' Danielle said without looking up from her phone.

Sunny could feel her nails making half moons in the palms of her hands. 'We've already got a voiceover.'

They were on their own in one of the studio rooms – rooms that were reserved for editing the films they were working on. Someone was coming round to check and help them later, but for now they were on their own.

Danielle let go of her phone long enough to reach back and pull her hair up into a ponytail. Sunny suspected she only did it because it made her boobs stick out more. She glanced at Will. Yep. He was staring at Danielle's chest.

'I don't mean the question–asking bits?' Danielle said. 'I mean a proper voiceover, describing what we're doing, you know? Like in a documentary.'

'I don't think we need that, do we?' Kitty said. 'Isn't

it going to be clear what the film's about by, um, the question?'

'I just thought we should make it as professional as possible?' Danielle said.

'Why don't we try it?' Will said. 'If it's not needed then we can get rid of it.'

'Exactly!' Danielle said. 'It's about trying things, isn't it? You never know what works until you try it.'

'And if you try it, you might like it,' Will said, grinning, and Danielle laughed.

Sunny turned to Hannah to roll her eyes, but Hannah was texting too. Sunny felt her phone buzz in her pocket. She thought about ignoring it – she'd just been judging the others after all – but she did feel a bit of a lemon, so she took it out. It was a photo of her dad – he was doing a sad face and holding a piece of paper with 'We never talk anymore . . .' written on it.

'That your dad?' Hannah asked.

'Yeah,' Sunny said, smiling. 'He's missing me.'

'He texts you?' Danielle said, looking up. 'Your dad?'

'Sunny's dad is so lovely,' Kitty said. 'He would've come with us if he could.'

'I'm surprised you were allowed to come, actually,' Danielle said, leaning forward in her chair, which gave everyone else a clear view down her top. 'I was shocked when I first saw you.'

'Why?' Sunny said, frowning.

'You know?' Danielle waved one hand over her head. 'Doesn't that mean you're really religious? So I didn't think you'd be allowed to come to something like this on your own.'

Even though Hannah and Kitty had said similar things. Even though Sunny had actually been surprised her parents had let her come, hearing Danielle say it really annoyed her.

'No, it doesn't mean I'm "really religious",' Sunny said, doing air quotes. 'It means I respect my religion, and I respect myself. Something I don't expect you to understand.'

'What's that supposed to mean?' Danielle said.

Sunny shook her head. 'Nothing. It doesn't matter.'

Will looked from Sunny to Danielle and back again. 'Let's just get on with editing this film, okay?'

'Okay,' Sunny said.

Danielle shrugged.

Will pressed some buttons and the laptop screen filled with the image of the park on the Embankment. At the start, the camera was pointing down at the ground.

'We can cut that,' Will said.

'You think?' Hannah said, grinning.

Then the camera was panning around the park. It looked great. The sun was shining, the grass was green, there was a tree covered with lush white flowers that Sunny had zoomed in and out of, catching every detail of the petals. Then she had filmed along the top of a beautiful white building and zoomed in on the various brightly coloured flags fluttering in the breeze. Just watching it – something she'd filmed – made Sunny's stomach flutter too.

Sunny had filmed outside the park too – the road, the river, the buildings on the opposite side.

'That's the South Bank Centre, isn't it?' Kitty said.

'Yeah,' Will said. 'There's a fairground there. They're taking us tomorrow, I think.'

'Oh yeah?' Hannah said. 'How do you know?'

Will tapped something on the keyboard. 'I heard Liz talking about it. To Steven.'

'Cool,' Kitty said.

While Will watched the film and Sunny, Hannah and Kitty made suggestions about how he might edit it, Danielle mostly stared at her phone. Any suggestions she made were just about her – mostly how she looked on camera – and since she'd disappeared from the park quite early on, there wasn't much for her to comment on.

'I'm gonna go, okay?' she said after an hour or so. 'You don't need me, do you? I said I'd meet someone at Top Shop.'

'I think we're supposed to do this together,' Kitty said, glancing at Sunny and Hannah.

'But there's nothing for me to do!' Danielle stood up. 'You guys have got it covered. I'll come back for the bit with the tutor. The proper editing bit.'

'No,' Sunny said. 'You don't get to pick and choose. If you're not going to take this seriously, we'll have to report you.'

'Hang on . . .' Will said.

'Oh, come on,' Danielle said. 'Don't be such a nerd! This is a summer course? It's supposed to be fun!'

'Maybe for you?' Sunny said. 'But I'm here to learn. I don't even know why you're here if you don't want to take part!'

She stood up, intending to storm out, but Hannah grabbed her arm.

'Let go,' Sunny said.

Her face was burning and her eyes were prickling. She really didn't want to cry in front of Danielle. Or Will.

'No,' Hannah said. 'Calm down. This is all getting out of hand and if you storm off, Danielle will go and it'll get worse. Just sit down.'

Sunny closed her eyes and allowed herself to be pulled back into one of the office-type chairs that were dotted around the room.

Kitty passed her a tissue and she took it without even looking up. She was so embarrassed she felt sick.

'So I'm going to go?' Danielle said.

'No!' Hannah almost shouted. 'You sit down too. We need to sort this out.'

Sunny looked up in time to see Danielle dramatically roll her eyes and drop back into a chair by the wall.

'I'm not good at this technical stuff,' Danielle said, waving a manicured hand over the equipment. 'I'm good at PR stuff. And presenting?'

'Okay,' Hannah said. 'And we have left you out a bit, you're right. It's just that we already knew each other.'

'You didn't know Will though,' Danielle said. 'Did you?'

Sunny wanted to say that Will was nice, but instead she wiped her face and tucked the tissue in her pocket.

'No, we met on the first night,' Will said. 'I think

maybe it's a bit harder for your four because you're sharing a room too. It can be difficult when you're spending so much time together.'

'You're right,' Kitty said. 'But I think we all need to try harder to get on.'

'Oh,' Will said, grinning. 'I was going to suggest someone swaps with me. I'm all on my own.'

'Nice try,' Hannah said as everyone – including Sunny and Danielle – laughed.

'So I think we can manage without you for the rest of the day,' Hannah told Danielle. 'You can go. To Top Shop. Or wherever.'

'Yay!' Danielle said. 'See you later.'

As she passed Sunny, she muttered, 'Lighten up a bit, yeah?'

Once Danielle had gone, they all sat in silence.

'We haven't got much more to do really,' Will said. 'How about we just finish editing the interviews – cropping the beginning and the end and tidying them up – and then we can put them together at the session with Jax.'

'Sounds good,' Hannah said.

Sunny stared down at her hands. The skin around her nails was bleeding, she'd have to remember to buy some plasters on the way back.

17

The South Bank was buzzing. Music was coming from every direction and people were queuing at street-food vans parked along the balustrade and taking photos of each other posed in front of the river or photo-bombing the fake-statue street entertainers.

'This is so cool,' Kitty said. 'Dylan would love this.'

She got out her phone and started taking photos and texting them.

It was ridiculously busy, but people moved out of the way when they saw Will's wheelchair.

'This is one of the advantages,' Will smiled. 'This chair's like a snow plough, but for people.'

Actually getting to the South Bank had been a pain – the route they'd taken from the dorm had led to some steps and they hadn't been able to find another option. In the end Will had walked down, holding on to the rail, while Joel carried his chair.

The entrance to the fair was via a path through

trees with multi-coloured paper lanterns hanging from the branches. It was like a grotto.

'This is gorgeous!' Kitty said. 'Let me get a photo.'

'I'll take one,' Will offered.

Sunny, Kitty and Hannah huddled together while Will took the photo.

'Want me to get one of all of you?' Liz said.

She'd been hanging back with them since she'd seen Joel carrying Will's chair. Sunny thought she probably felt guilty for not realising their route hadn't been accessible for him. Either that or she was worrying Will would make a complaint.

Will handed Liz the phone and wheeled himself round to the girls.

'*Charlie's Angels* pose, please,' Will said, and then had to show them what he meant, since none of them knew what he was talking about. It was basically making finger-guns.

'I can't believe you don't know *Charlie's Angels*,' Will grumbled as they headed into the fair. 'It's a classic.'

'Has it got Cameron Diaz in it?' Hannah said.

'God, not that one!' Will said, putting his head in his hands. 'I'm talking about the original TV show, not the remake. I'll send you a DVD when we get home.'

'So, where first?' Kitty said as they all moved out of the way of the next lot of people coming in.

'I want to go on the roller coaster,' Hannah said, pointing. The roller coaster was small but twisty and they could hear people screaming even from the opposite side of the fair.

'Ugh, go for it,' Sunny said. 'I don't. I'll wait here with Will.'

'But I'm going on it!' Will said.

Sunny gasped with embarrassment. 'Oh! Sorry, I –'

'I'm joking,' Will said.

Hannah and Kitty ran off to join the queue.

'I was always desperate to go on roller coasters when I was little,' Will said. 'And then my mum took me to Alton Towers – she'd saved up for it for ages – and we went on one there. It wasn't even a big scary one, it was pretty basic. And I absolutely hated it. I thought I was going to be sick, and when we got off, I went and pretended to throw up so I could cry without my mum seeing.'

'That's so sad!' Sunny said.

'It wasn't so bad,' Will said. 'My poor mum though.'

'My mum loves the fair,' Sunny said. 'It's weird because usually she hates a lot of noise and she's always worrying about us, but when the fair comes to our local park, she's worse than my little brother. She loves the waltzers. And my dad gets really evil on the dodgems.'

Will laughed. 'I've never been on the waltzers. Just looking at them makes me feel sick. You hungry?'

Sunny and Will weaved through the crowd to a food van at the edge of the fair. It turned out to be selling crêpes – Will got Nutella and Sunny got raspberry jam. They carried them over to a nearby bench – the couple sitting there were just finishing up and actually got up quicker once they saw Will.

They sat in silence while Sunny waved away the wasps that kept trying to dive-bomb her jam. She looked out across the fair and thought of all the times she'd been to the local one with her parents. Her dad had actually taken her mum to a fair on one of their first dates, so every time it came to town they all had to rush down there and spend at least a day trying out every ride and as much of the food as they could. Aisha had even gone on the Wall of Death – the big spinning drum where you stand up and you're not even strapped in – last time. She'd loved it, but Sunny's dad hadn't even been able to look.

Sunny usually stuck to the basic rides, like taking Hamzah on the kiddie roller coaster or maybe joining her dad on the bumper cars. She never even considered the full-on ones like the crane with the swinging arm, or the tower with the seats that dropped down. Just the thought of them made her feel a bit sick and dizzy.

Will said something, but Sunny didn't hear. She turned to him and leaned closer.

'You don't have to look after me,' he said, his mouth near her ear.

Her stomach flipped over. She shook her head. 'I'm not.'

'I mean, if you'd wanted to go on the Cyclone thing with Hannah and Kitty, you should've done. I'm cool on my own. Honest.' He smiled.

'No, I didn't, honestly. I'm fine sitting here with you.'

Will grinned. 'As long as you don't feel like you have to be responsible for me or keep me entertained or anything. I get enough of that from . . .' He shook his head.

'Your mum?' Sunny said. 'No, it's not that, honestly. I like you. You're funny.'

'I am, aren't I?'

'And so modest.' Sunny grinned.

'And I like you too,' Will said. 'You just looked very . . .' He pulled a miserable face.

'Oh, I'm sorry!' Sunny dropped the last of her crêpe in the nearest bin. 'It's not you. I was thinking about my parents.'

'You don't get on with them?' Will asked.

Sunny shook her head. 'It's not that. They're great. But . . . Don't say anything to Hannah or Kitty, okay?'

Will nodded.

'We're moving. Down here, actually. They told me just before I left.'

'Ah,' Will said. 'That sucks.'

'Yeah,' Sunny said. 'It does.'

'Have you told your boyfriend?' Will said.

Sunny looked down at her hands and then curled them into fists to hide the bits she'd picked at. She thought about telling Will that she wasn't really going out with Sam, that she'd made it up. But then she'd have to tell him why she didn't want to go out with him and she didn't want to have to do that. Assuming that he even wanted to go out with her, that is. It was easier just to lie.

She shook her head. 'No. Not yet.'

'That's going to be hard,' Will said.

'Yep.' Sunny looked out across the fair again. 'Hey, is that Hannah and Kitty?' She pointed over at the Cyclone.

The two girls were waving frantically from their seats. Sunny noticed Joel and Dillon were sitting behind them. Sunny waved back.

'Is there anything here you want to go on?' she asked Will.

Will grinned. 'Yeah. But I don't think you'll want to join me.'

'What?'

Without even looking, he pointed straight up. Sunny tipped her head back and even with the sun in her eyes she could see a swing, high, high above everything. Higher than the surrounding buildings. The swings were flying out at the side like a twirling skirt.

'Oh no.'

'See. I knew you wouldn't want to.'

'It's so high! Why would you even –'

'Imagine the view! It'd be like being a bird!'

'How about the London Eye?' Sunny suggested. 'That's really high. But you're actually in a pod, so –'

'So it's not the same. You're protected. There's glass between you and everything else.'

'That's good. That means you probably won't die.'

Will laughed. 'You won't die on that either. Probably.'

'Very reassuring.' Sunny looked up again. No. It was way too high.

'You're strapped in and everything.'

'I would think!'

'It looks amazing,' Will said.

'It looks terrifying.'

She looked up again. It was stupidly high. Her stomach felt fluttery just looking at it. Nope. Not doing it.

'No problem. I can go on my own.' He did a sad puppy face.

'Oh, please,' Sunny said. 'As if you're going to guilt me into it. Especially since you've just finished telling me you're fine on your own, you don't need anyone.'

'It's true,' he said. 'I'm a lone wolf.' He tipped his head back and howled.

18

Sunny went to pray and when she had finished she didn't feel like going back to the fair immediately – it looked even busier than before and the weather had certainly got hotter – so she got a cup of cloudy lemonade and walked along the Embankment until she found a low wall to sit on. There were benches, but they were all piled with people – either families with hot and over-excited kids in buggies, or couples wrapped around one another or tensely staring at their phones.

Sunny tipped her head back to feel the sun on her face and then looked out over the river. She thought about the river at home and the view on the other side. She thought about moving to Richmond, being nearer her family – she always had a great time with her cousins, but maybe it was because they didn't see each other very often – but then she thought about being away from Kitty and Hannah.

She didn't want to leave. But being near London might be good. And Kitty and Hannah could always visit.

She reached into her bag and took out the course camera – in the last lesson she'd asked if she could borrow it to practise with over the weekend – and filmed a sweeping shot along the river. Then she finished her drink, and headed back to the fair and the crowds.

There were all kinds of people there – and a lot more Asians than Sunny was used to seeing at home. Women in niqab and boys in trainers and, despite the heat, hoodies, with stuff shaved into their short hair. It reminded her a bit of an Asian market they'd all gone to once years ago. It made her wish her family was with her. Hamzah would love it.

She walked up to the door of the Victorian circus and peered inside. It was dark and looked cool, but she didn't want to go in on her own, so she kept walking. She walked around the back of the roller coaster Kitty and Hannah had been on – covering her ears against the loud rattling of the cars on the tracks. It brought her out next to a high fence with a gate leading to the Secret Garden.

When she stepped through the gate, Sunny knew she'd have to find Kitty and Hannah and bring them back to show them. It was so beautiful. Around the sides were huge plants with bright orange flowers that looked like flames and in the centre was a fountain, the water changing colour as it bubbled over rocks. At the far end, in the shade, there were benches with arches over the top and pink roses climbing up and hanging down. Sunny walked around the central fountain, wondering whether she should take a photo to send home or whether to wait and take one with Hannah and Kitty. She was just about to text Kitty to tell them to come and find her when she saw them.

Not Hannah and Kitty. Will. And Danielle. Danielle was sitting on one of the benches, her sunglasses pushed up on her head and a big smile on her face. Will was in his chair in front of her, leaning towards her and he was smiling too.

Sunny stepped back towards the gate. She knew she should have left them to it. It was none of her business what they were doing, she barely knew either of them. But she couldn't make herself leave. She didn't want to. She wanted to watch them.

Danielle shook her head, her blond hair falling down her back. Will rubbed the back of his neck, pulling his shoulders back. Danielle copied him, pulling her shoulders back and pushing her chest out. She was wearing a V-neck T-shirt and Sunny could see the lace of her bra through it. Danielle leaned forward and put her hands on Will's thighs. Sunny could hear him laugh from where she was standing. She told herself to leave. It was obvious what was about to happen. Will leaned even further forward. And then they were kissing. So much for him being a 'lone wolf'.

Sunny watched for long enough to see one of Will's hands start to make its way under Danielle's T-shirt and then she made herself walk away. At the gate she stopped and turned back. She still had her phone in her hand and without really knowing why, she snapped a quick picture of the two of them and then pushed her way back into the crowd.

19

Everyone met at the gate at the arranged time. Sunny didn't want to walk back with Will and Danielle, so she hung back a bit and waited for Kitty and Hannah to come and find her. Kitty came, but Hannah was walking with Joel.

'You okay?' Kitty asked Sunny.

'Yeah, just tired,' Sunny said. She really was tired. She felt like she could climb into her bed as soon as they got back to the dorm. 'Did you have a good time?'

'Yeah,' Kitty said. 'I just got a bit fed up of everyone asking me about Dylan all the time.'

'Really?'

Kitty nodded. 'Yeah, everyone's really interested in me being gay.'

'They were okay about it though?' Sunny asked. 'No one was –'

'No no,' Kitty interrupted. 'Everyone was nice. It's

just . . . it freaks me out a bit cos it's always going to be a thing, you know?'

Kitty stopped and leaned on the rail at the side of the bridge. 'People talk about coming out as if it's a one-off, you know? Big announcement and that's it. But really you have to keep coming out all the time. For your whole life.'

'Wow,' Sunny said, looking along the river towards Big Ben and the London Eye. 'I never thought of it like that.'

'I remember Tom saying it – or something like that – ages ago,' Kitty said. 'But I didn't really think about it. You don't, do you, until it happens to you? I mean, every new person I ever meet is going to assume I have a boyfriend not a girlfriend, right?'

'Probably,' Sunny said. 'It's a bit like people assuming I'm white if we've only talked on the phone or whatever.'

'Yeah,' Kitty said. 'It's rubbish.'

They both sighed and then Kitty laughed. 'State of us. Look where we are and we're feeling sorry for ourselves!'

Sunny turned and looked down the river in the other direction, towards St Paul's Cathedral, Tower Bridge and the Gherkin.

'I saw Will kissing Danielle,' she said.

'Oh my god,' Kitty said. 'Really?'

Sunny nodded. 'In the Secret Garden near the Cyclone. She was all over him.'

'Wow,' Kitty said. 'I wouldn't have put those two together.'

'Me neither,' Sunny said. She looked along the bridge and realised the rest of the group were almost on the Strand.

'We'd better catch up,' she said.

When they got back to the dorm, Sunny went straight into the bathroom and shut the door. Danielle wasn't there, of course. She'd probably gone back to Will's room with him. Sunny ran the taps and cleaned her teeth almost ferociously, staring at herself in the mirror. She changed into her pyjamas and sat on the loo to read her texts.

Sam had sent her a picture of a guinea pig wearing glasses. She deleted it. Her dad had sent a long message about his day and ended it saying he was looking forward to talking to her later. She deleted that too. And then she felt guilty and tried to get it back, but it was too late.

'Sun?' Kitty said as Sunny walked back in the

room and climbed the ladder to her bed. 'Are you sure you're okay?'

'I'm fine.' She flopped back on her pillows. 'Really.'

'Kitty told me what happened,' Hannah said. 'It was probably just a kiss. It doesn't mean –'

'It doesn't matter!' Sunny said. 'I don't like him like that. Stop going on about it.'

'It just doesn't seem fair that your parents –' Hannah started to say.

Sunny sat up. 'It's got nothing to do with my parents. You don't even know what you're talking about. How many times have I told you that I'm not interested? I don't get why you don't believe me.'

'Er, because you're acting like this?' Hannah said. 'But, you know, whatever, if you want to pretend you're not fussed that's fine. I'm not bothered.'

'Good,' Sunny said. 'I'm going to sleep. Try not to be too loud on FaceTime, okay?'

Sunny couldn't get to sleep. Her head felt fizzy with thoughts and worries. She was back at the fair, wandering around on her own, looking across the river, standing in the entrance of the Secret Garden, seeing Danielle with Will. She took her phone out from under her pillow and opened her photos.

Danielle's hands on Will's legs. Will pressed up as close to Danielle as he could get. She swiped to enlarge it and scrolled around, looking at every detail. Danielle was wearing hoop earrings. She had a mole on her shoulder. Will's hair was cut perfectly straight across his neck. Sunny could see the outline of the label of his T-shirt. She stared at their mouths, pressed together and wondered what it felt like. What it would feel like to kiss Will like that?

Shaking her head, she deleted the photo and shoved her phone back under her pillow. She was wigging out, she knew. She wished she were at home so she could talk to her sister. Even though she was older than Sunny and had more friends and more of a life, Aisha was cool with the move because she'd met a boy. She hadn't said anything to Sunny, but after their parents had told them about the planned move – after Sunny had stormed out and up to her bedroom – Aisha had gone to talk to her.

To begin with, she'd said it was about being near to family, but Sunny hadn't been convinced.

'There's a boy, right?' Sunny had said. 'You've met someone.'

Aisha shook her head, but she always did this fake wide-eyed thing when she was lying.

'Who is he?' Sunny said. 'Either you've met someone here you want to get away from or there's someone down there you want to get to know better.'

'You know me too well,' Aisha said. She'd pulled her hair out of its hairband and started brushing it, looking at herself in the mirror.

'Come on,' Sunny said. 'Do I look like an idiot?'

Aisha looked at her in the mirror and grinned.

'Shut up,' Sunny said and smiled. 'Do I know him?'

Aisha swung round on the stool. 'You haven't met him. He's a friend of Ruksana's.'

Ruksana was one of their cousins. She was the one everyone else looked up to. She was studying politics at university and worked really hard, but she was also the one everyone wanted to be at the family parties because she was such a good laugh.

'And?' Sunny asked.

'He's really handsome. And he's funny. He's at UCL studying law. We got talking because he volunteers at a food bank too. He's called Adam.'

'He's Muslim, right?' Sunny said, frowning.

'Of course!' Aisha said, shaking her head. 'God, Sunny!'

Sunny held her hands up. 'Okay. I was only asking. So you like him?'

'Yeah.' She grinned. 'And all evening, every time I looked at him, he was looking at me. We went to that ice-cream place you know? Olives & Lemons? And he put some music on the jukebox. He just seems really nice.'

'What does Ruksana say?'

'About him? She says he's perfect for me.'

'Why isn't she interested?'

'Because she likes someone else. And she says she doesn't fancy him.'

'So you're happy to go? To move hundreds of miles away? What if he's not interested? What if it turns out you don't like him after all? And then we're stuck down there.'

'God, Sun, we'll be with our family! It's not like they're moving us somewhere like Qatar!'

'Yeah, you say that. What's to stop them? If we go along with this, what if Dad suddenly gets an offer somewhere else and they move us again?'

'You know they wouldn't do that,' Aisha said.

'Do I?' Sunny shook her head. 'I didn't know they would do this! It's okay for you, you could refuse if you wanted to. You could get a job and go and live on your own. I have to do whatever they decide. I don't really have a choice at all. It's not fair.'

Aisha rolled her eyes. 'Life's not fair.'

'Now you sound like Mum.'

'It's true though. It could be a lot worse. You should come to the food bank with me, that'd shut you up. You've got a face on because your family – who love you – want to move to a better area with a better job and live in a better house close to more family who love you. Boo hoo.'

Sunny knew Aisha was right. She knew things could be a lot worse. But did that really mean she just had to accept everything? You can't complain about anything – anything at all – because someone has it worse than you? That didn't seem right. There would always, always be someone worse off, same as there was always someone better off.

20

Sunny's body seemed to react to the alarm before her mind even realised what was happening. She was halfway down the ladder of the bunk bed before her brain found the words 'fire alarm'.

'What the hell?' she heard Hannah say.

'Fire alarm,' she mumbled. 'Kitty?'

'I'm getting up,' Kitty said, her voice croaky.

'Can't we just wait and see if it stops?' Hannah asked.

'No,' Sunny said, pulling her hoodie on over her pyjamas. She turned back towards her own bed. 'Danielle?'

There was no movement so Sunny called her name again and then, when there was still no response, went over and shook the duvet.

'She's not here,' Sunny said, her stomach lurching with fear.

'Who? Danielle?' Kitty said.

'Yeah,' Sunny said. 'Her bed's empty.'

'Bloody hell,' Hannah said. She'd climbed down the ladder now and joined Sunny in feeling around Danielle's bed.

Kitty switched on the light and they blinked at the brightness.

'No,' Kitty said. 'She's definitely not there.'

Hannah said, 'You don't think she's with –'

All three girls jumped as someone hammered on the door of the room.

'Come on!' a male voice shouted. 'Everyone out!'

Hannah opened the door to see Steven, looking tired, dishevelled and panicked.

'Is it a real fire?' Hannah asked him.

'I don't know,' Steven said. 'But you have to get out. Go on. Don't use the lift.'

'Danielle's not here,' Sunny said. 'She's not in her bed.'

Steven had moved along to the next door – a smaller room that Sarah shared with Miyuki – banging on it and shouting.

'Do you know where she is?' Steven asked Sunny.

'She might be with Will,' she said.

Steven frowned and shook his head, and then Sarah opened the door and Steven pushed them all past to join the other bleary-eyed students heading for the stairs.

The stone steps were freezing under Sunny's feet and she could feel herself trembling. She wrapped her arms around herself under her hoodie.

'How's Will going to get out if he can't use the lift?' Sunny said.

'Oh my god,' Hannah said.

'There must be a way,' Kitty said. 'It wouldn't be legal not to.'

'I'm going back up,' Sunny said, turning and starting to push her way through the students following them.

'No,' Kitty said. 'You can't.' She grabbed Sunny's hand. 'We'll ask someone when we get downstairs, but you can't go back up.'

'Steven's still there,' Hannah said. 'He'll get him if he's not out already.'

Sunny nodded. It didn't feel right, leaving without knowing Will was safe, but she knew she shouldn't go back to a fire, they'd learned that on a first-aid course at school.

Pretty much everyone else had passed them now, there were just a few stragglers, so it was hard to get down the stairs, and there was practically a bottleneck at the front door.

'This is not safe,' Sunny said. The back of her neck prickled with fear.

They'd made it to the bottom of the stairs, but they were still in the lobby when they heard the sirens.

Sunny felt like she was going to be sick. 'What if Will's still up there?'

She felt Kitty grab her hand. 'They won't have left until they'd made sure he was okay. I bet he's outside with Steven right now. Don't worry.'

The three of them finally managed to make it out into the street, where some people from the other floors – people they hadn't seen before, didn't even know were there – were standing around in their onesies, no make-up, hair all over the place. Joel looked much younger without his massive black-rimmed glasses and Sarah with the blue hair had put her coat on over her pyjamas and was leaning against the shoulder of another girl, her eyes closed.

'It's okay,' Kitty said, pulling on Sunny's arm. 'Look. There he is.'

She pointed just a bit further along the street. Will was sitting on the floor, leaning back against the front of the building next door. Liz was standing beside him, phone in hand, her face strained.

Sunny's breath caught in her chest and she pulled away from Kitty and walked over to Will. The pavement was cold and gritty under her bare feet.

'Hey,' she said.

Will was wearing tracksuit bottoms and a grey T-shirt. Two walking sticks lay on the ground beside him. Sunny noticed the muscles in his arms. And then she noticed she was looking at his arms because she was avoiding looking at his face. She made herself do it. She smiled.

'You okay?' he said.

He looked different. He wasn't smiling. He looked like he was in pain.

'We weren't sure you'd got out,' she said, running her hand over her hood to make sure her head was covered.

'Yeah, it's amazing what adrenaline can do.' He smiled. 'Nice pyjamas.'

Sunny looked down at her pink-and-white striped pyjama bottoms.

'They're my best ones,' she said. 'I always wear them when I think I'm going to be chucked out of bed in the middle of the night.'

And then Will smiled, and Sunny found that she wanted to cry.

'They don't think there's really a fire,' Will said.

'No,' Sunny said. 'I –'

She was interrupted by the fire engine pulling up right next to them – the breeze it caused made everyone's hair flutter. The crowd cleared to allow the three firefighters who jumped down from the fire engine to walk through and inside the building.

'They got through the crowd a lot quicker than us,' Kitty noted.

She was right behind Sunny. Sunny hadn't even realised she was there.

'They're carrying axes,' Hannah said. 'Plus they're totally hot.'

Sunny rolled her eyes and Will grinned at her.

'Danielle not with you?' he said.

Sunny first felt a punch of disappointment. Of course he was asking about Danielle. Of course he was more interested in her than he was in Sunny – why wouldn't he be? And then her stomach clenched with panic.

Where was Danielle?

21

Steven looked exhausted. His hair was sticking up in tufts and his glasses couldn't hide the purple smudges under his eyes. He kept sitting down next to Liz – who also looked pale and tired – and then standing up and pacing in front of the windows in the common room. For once almost everyone was quiet, although Sunny could hear someone tapping on their phone.

'The person responsible,' Steven said, as though everyone didn't already know it was Danielle, 'will be disciplined. But I wanted to reiterate that there is no smoking in this building. And that means no smoking. And, no, you can't go outside to smoke. In the first instance, we will contact the parents of anyone found smoking. And if it happens again, we will ask them to leave the course.'

Steven sat down, crossed one leg over the other knee, pulled at his sock and then stood up again.

'Obviously the same thing applies to drinking,' Steven said. 'Anyone found drinking – or even in possession of – alcohol will be asked to leave.'

'So has Danielle been chucked out?' Hannah whispered in Sunny's ear.

Sunny shook her head. She didn't know. She assumed so, based on what Steven was saying, but Danielle was back in their room, where she'd been since the firefighters had found her drunk and asleep on the communal bathroom floor the previous night, so Sunny wasn't sure.

'What happened last night,' Steven said, 'must not happen again. Everyone in the building was put at risk.' His hand hovered around Liz's shoulder, then he folded his arm. 'I'm very disappointed.'

When the three of them got back to their room, Danielle was out of bed and rummaging through her bag. She looked terrible. Her hair was up in a ponytail, but looked dirty and ragged, she was wearing a hoodie with frayed wrists, but her legs were bare.

'Are you okay?' Kitty asked her.

'Yeah,' Danielle said, 'I just need to sort some stuff out.'

'Are you packing?' Hannah asked. 'Are you leaving?'

Danielle shrugged. 'I don't know. They've called my parents, but . . .' She pulled at a loose thread on her sleeve.

The four of them stood looking at each other.

'So you can have your bottom bunk back,' Danielle said to Sunny.

'Good,' Sunny said. 'Thanks.'

Danielle stared at her. Sunny couldn't work out the expression on her face, but it made her feel guilty and then angry for feeling guilty. She hadn't done anything wrong, had she? It had all been Danielle.

'What is your problem?' Danielle asked her.

Sunny noticed she had yesterday's make-up smudged around her eyes.

'I don't have a problem,' Sunny said.

'Come on, spit it out,' Danielle said. 'You're obviously pissed off.'

'We're just leaving,' Kitty said. 'Sunny?'

'Yeah, go,' Danielle said. 'Run along together.' She turned back to her bag and Sunny couldn't help herself.

'We spent half the night standing outside in the cold because you couldn't make it through the night without a cigarette!' Sunny said. 'That's my problem. Will went downstairs with his stick and he was in a lot of pain. The college is going to have to pay for the fire brigade coming out – did Steven tell you that? All because of you. And you're not even sorry.'

'Sunny,' Kitty said. 'Come on.'

'That's not your problem,' Danielle said. 'You've had a problem with me since I first walked in here. I know you thought you'd have the room to yourself – you and your coven – that you wouldn't need to talk to any of the other plebs on the course, but tough luck. There are four beds in here so, you know, deal. But it's not just that. You look at me like I'm a piece of crap.'

'I do?' Sunny said. She could feel her throat getting tight. 'The first time you saw me, you looked me up and down and decided I wasn't worth bothering with.'

Danielle laughed, shaking her head. 'Yeah? But that's exactly what you did to me. You're still doing it now! You think I don't see the way you look at me? Just because you have to cover yourself up from head to toe, doesn't mean we all should.'

Sunny couldn't remember the last time she'd been so angry. She actually wanted to slap Danielle. Instead, she grabbed hold of the edge of the bed.

'I don't have to cover myself up. You don't know what you're talking about. I *choose* this. I choose to cover my head out of respect, something I don't expect you to understand.'

Danielle smirked. 'Yeah, you said. I'm sure that's what you tell yourself. But I'm sorry, I can't believe you'd choose to dress like that. As if any teenage girl would. And just because you're jealous, doesn't mean you should judge other people. I'm comfortable with my body. I like the way I look. I'm happy in my clothes.'

'You don't dress for yourself!' Sunny said. 'You dress like that so boys will look at you. It's disgusting.'

'Ah,' Danielle said, rubbing one foot against the back of her leg. 'So that's what this is really about.'

'What?' Sunny said. She wanted to leave. She wanted to slam the door in Danielle's smug face.

'Will.' Danielle shrugged.

'It's got nothing to do with Will,' Sunny said. Her breath was coming too fast.

'Yeah, right,' Danielle said. 'It's so obvious that you like him. You've been all over him since we got here. I don't know how that fits with –' she waved her hand at Sunny as if to indicate the modesty of her clothes – 'especially since you've got a boyfriend. Is that about respecting your religion too?'

'What boyfriend?' Sunny heard Hannah say.

'Oh?' Danielle said and grinned. 'It's a secret boyfriend? You haven't told your precious friends? Why's that then? Someone you shouldn't be seeing? He's not one of *their* boyfriends, is he? You don't look like a boyfriend stealer, but they do say it's the quiet ones –'

'I haven't got a boyfriend!' Sunny shouted. 'I haven't got a boyfriend. I've never had a boyfriend. I don't want a boyfriend. I like Will, yes. And I thought he liked me. No, he does like me. I know he does. And, yeah, I was upset when I saw him with you, but that's because I don't like you. I think he could do better and I was disappointed that he fell for your –' She waved her hand at Danielle in the same way Danielle had done it to her.

'Oh yeah?' Danielle said, laughing. 'How sad are you? I've had enough of this.'

She stepped into her flip-flops and walked out of the room.

22

Sunny felt dazed. She only started to come round when Hannah put a mug of hot chocolate in front of her.

'Are you okay?' Kitty asked her.

'I don't understand what just happened,' Sunny said. 'It was like I was outside my body.'

'I felt like that when I had that row with Mackenzie in the park,' Kitty said. 'I was shaking afterwards, remember?'

Sunny held out her hands in front of her. The were trembling wildly. 'I think I'm going to be sick.'

'You're not,' Hannah said. 'Drink your hot chocolate.'

'Isn't it too hot?'

'It's out of the machine. It's probably not even warm.'

Sunny took a sip. It was hot enough that some steam drifted up her nose, but not so hot that it burned her tongue. And it was surprisingly nice. She closed her eyes and felt the warmth run down inside her.

'I don't think I've ever seen you so angry before,' Kitty said.

'I feel terrible,' Sunny said. 'What did I even say?'

'You want a recap?' Hannah asked.

'Ugh.' Sunny drank some more chocolate. 'Not yet, no. Let me finish this first. I feel like I need to sleep.'

'It's the adrenaline wearing off,' Hannah said.

'How do you know so much about this?' Sunny asked her.

'Er, hello?' Hannah said. 'I'm usually the drama queen of the group.'

Sunny looked at Hannah for the first time since they'd left the room. Hannah looked bright-eyed and pink-cheeked and Sunny wanted to hug her for being such a good friend. It wasn't a feeling she was really used to.

Sunny smiled. 'Maybe we're taking it in turns. Kitty had a go at Mackenzie, now I've had a go at Danielle. You're next.'

Hannah shrugged. 'I've had hundreds of massive rows since Kitty's Mackenzie thing.'

'I don't know how you do it,' Sunny said. 'I feel

like I want to bury myself in a hole. Actually, can we go to that park?'

'You're not going to bury yourself, Sun. We've got the day off!' Kitty said.

'Drink your chocolate,' Hannah repeated. 'And then we'll go out and find some breakfast and you can tell us what that was all about.'

'Ugh,' Sunny said, resisting the urge to just lay her head down on the table. She drank slowly, waiting for her heart rate to come back down. Her friends sat in silence – Hannah was texting – and sipped their own drinks and Sunny was grateful. She didn't want to talk right now. She really didn't want to talk about Will. Or Danielle. But she knew she'd feel better once she had talked to them. She also knew she was going to feel like a complete idiot. She downed the rest of her drink, even the horrible powdery bit at the bottom.

When they left the dorm, they walked down the street opposite – the workmen were gone – and through the park. Kitty linked arms with Sunny.

'Don't worry,' Sunny said. 'I'm not really going to bury myself in a hole. It's tempting though.'

'You just need a good breakfast,' Kitty said. 'And a good chat.'

'I should've talked to you two before,' Sunny said. 'I don't know why I didn't really.'

'I was the same when I first met Dylan,' Kitty said. 'Some things are hard to bring up. Even with good friends.'

'I know,' Sunny said. 'But I've been freaking out a bit. There's so many things I need to tell you.'

'Is here okay?' Hannah said, pointing.

It was a café in a small building. Raised above the park and set back from the Embankment, with seats outside on a sunny terrace overlooking the river. And it looked almost empty.

'Perfect,' Sunny said.

Sunny sat outside with Kitty, while Hannah went inside to order for them all.

'I think she's enjoying herself,' Sunny said, smiling at Kitty.

'You know she loves drama,' Kitty said. 'But are you okay? Really?'

Sunny nodded. 'Yeah. But I'm going to have to apologise to Danielle, which I'm not looking forward to . . .'

'You might not,' Kitty said. 'Not if she really does get chucked out.'

Sunny frowned. 'I want to apologise though.

She was right. I totally judged her because of her clothes.'

'She did the same to you though,' Kitty said. 'You were right about that.'

Sunny nodded. 'So stupid. She judged me for covering up and I judged her for not being covered up enough. Is there a right amount of clothes that means you don't get judged?'

'I don't think so,' Kitty said. 'Then you get called frumpy. Or a tomboy.'

'Ugh,' Sunny said. 'It's ridiculous. Has it always been like this?'

Kitty shrugged. 'I think maybe it's getting worse? Mum says it is, but I don't know for sure.'

Hannah came back out carrying three huge mugs with steam curling from the froth on the top. 'Lattes,' she announced. 'I just got one shot for both of you. Kitty cos she's a wuss, Sunny cos I don't think caffeine's your friend right now.'

She sat down and scooted her chair around a bit so she was facing Sunny.

'So,' she said. 'Tell us everything.'

'Oh god,' Sunny said. 'Okay. So, the first thing is that my parents are moving down here. To Richmond.'

Hannah and Kitty both stared at her.

Kitty said, 'Oh no! Sunny!'

Hannah said, 'Why do they want to do that?'

'I know,' Sunny said. 'Dad's going into partnership with Uncle Ibrahim.'

'When?' Kitty said.

Sunny shook her head. 'I don't know exactly, but soon. They've found a house. And I know what they're like when they have a plan.'

Hannah snorted. 'Obviously where you get it from.'

Sunny nodded. 'I know, right?'

'But . . .' Kitty said. 'But when will we see you?'

Sunny looked out across the river and blinked in the sun. 'We'll be coming back a lot. So they say. Cos, you know, we've still got family up there. But I don't know.'

'Maybe it won't really happen,' Kitty said. 'Maybe something will go wrong. I mean, I'm not saying I want something to go wrong . . .'

'No, I know,' Sunny said. 'I've been thinking the same thing. And you never know. My dad's been talking about doing this for so long and it's never actually happened. So fingers crossed.'

'We would really miss you!' Kitty said.

Sunny's eyes welled with tears. 'I'd really miss you too.'

Hannah ripped open a sugar sachet and tipped it into her coffee. 'You can't go. You'll just have to convince them that it would be too damaging to your studies – they're really big on you going to uni, right?'

Sunny nodded.

'So tell them it's a crucial point. You can go after GCSEs but not before.'

'They know that though. They say the school in Richmond is better and that it'll be easy for me to catch up. Or whatever. They've talked to my cousins and I think my mum might have been in and talked to the Head already. It's a done deal.'

'It can't be,' Kitty said. 'Not if you refuse to go.'

'I'm not going to refuse to go,' Sunny said. 'I can explain why I don't want to go – they're not stupid, they know I don't want to leave you guys – but I can't say no.'

'Why not?' Hannah said.

Sunny shook her head. 'It's about respect. I trust that they are doing what's best for us as a family and what's best for me.'

'But parents don't always know best,' Hannah said. 'Look at my mum! She's never even home.'

'Because she's trying to make a better life for you!' Sunny said.

Hannah scoffed. 'That's what she says, yeah. But when's the better life going to happen?'

They were interrupted by a man bringing out their breakfasts. Full English for Kitty and Hannah and scrambled egg on toast for Sunny.

'Is that okay?' Hannah asked her.

'Perfect,' Sunny said.

Her stomach rumbled and she shoved a chunk of toast and egg in her mouth.

'I've just thought of something,' Hannah said through a mouthful of sausage. 'You could stay with me!'

Sunny stopped with her fork halfway to her mouth. Could she really do that? Would her parents agree to that? No. They wouldn't.

'They'd never go for that,' she said. And shoved the food in.

'You don't know that!' Kitty said. 'It's worth asking, right? It would be so good!'

'They feel really sorry for me being on my own so much, you know they do!' Hannah said.

'They do,' Sunny said. 'But they're much more likely to want you to come and live with us than to let me go and live with you.'

'Oh yeah,' Hannah said. 'If they think it's bad for

me they're not going to want the same for you.'

'Exactly,' Sunny said. 'Sorry.'

'Still,' Hannah said. 'Worth asking.'

'Definitely,' Sunny agreed. But she really didn't think it was.

They ate some more of their breakfasts and drank their lattes and Sunny started to feel better. She closed her eyes and turned her face up to the sun. It was funny how sometimes things that seemed completely out of control, totally overwhelming, could just suddenly almost fade away.

'So tell us about your boyfriend then,' Hannah said.

'Shut up,' Sunny growled.

Hannah laughed. 'No, really. Is it Sam?'

'Yes,' Sunny said, shoving some more toast in her mouth. 'My imaginary boyfriend is Sam.'

'Sam's not imaginary!' Kitty said, giggling. 'I've met him!'

Sunny pulled a face. 'He's been texting me a bit.'

'Sexts?!' Hannah shrieked.

Sunny shushed her, even though there wasn't anyone else around.

'No! Nothing like that. Just sort of cute jokes really.'

'Aw, he's flirting,' Kitty said.

'Yeah, I think so,' Sunny said.

'Show us!' Hannah said.

'What?' Sunny yelped.

'Show us the texts! And we'll tell you if he's flirting or not.'

Sunny shook her head. 'He's definitely flirting.'

'I definitely want to see,' Hannah said.

'I've deleted them,' Sunny lied.

She'd deleted some, but couldn't bear to get rid of a couple of them. They made her laugh.

'Why would you do that?' Hannah said.

'Her parents,' Kitty said.

'Yes, my parents,' Sunny said. 'But not the way you think. It's not about me hiding anything from them. I know I let you think that I'm not allowed a boyfriend. That it's all about my parents. But it's not. I just wouldn't . . . do anything like that. Unless it was serious.'

'But how do you know if it could be serious unless you, you know, try them out?' Hannah asked.

Sunny slurped her latte. 'No, I don't mean a serious relationship. I mean properly serious. I mean unless we were going to get married.'

Hannah and Kitty stared at her and she felt her face get hot. This was why she'd never wanted to tell them. They were looking at her like she was a total freak.

'Sunny,' Hannah said. 'You're fourteen!'

'I know,' Sunny said. 'But that's the way it is.'

'But . . .' Kitty said. 'Why?'

'Out of respect for my religion,' Sunny said.

'I never really thought of you as religious,' Hannah said.

Sunny laughed and pointed at her headscarf. 'Really?'

Hannah smiled, sheepishly. 'I kind of just always assumed it was down to your parents. I didn't think it was something so important to you.'

'It is though,' Sunny said. 'Does that weird you out? Do you think I'm a freak?'

'No!' Kitty said. 'Of course not.'

'No more than we already did,' Hannah said, bumping Sunny with her arm. 'I can't imagine it, but if it's important to you . . .'

'It is,' Sunny said.

'So you told Will you were seeing Sam rather than tell him all that?' Kitty asked.

'I thought that was better than telling him I like him, but we can't go out unless we're planning to get married,' Sunny grinned.

Hannah laughed. 'Can you imagine? He can move pretty fast in that wheelchair.'

'You like him though?' Kitty asked. 'Will?'

'I like them both!' Sunny said. 'I like Sam and Will. But I don't like them like that, you know?'

They sat in silence for a couple of minutes. Sunny listened to the traffic on the Embankment and Big Ben chiming eleven o'clock.

'Do you think I'm a total slapper?' Hannah said suddenly. 'I mean cos I'm still with Louis, officially, but I'm sort of seeing Joel . . .'

Sunny snorted. 'Of course not! This is about me not anyone else!'

'But what about Danielle?' Hannah said.

Sunny drained the last of her latte. 'Ugh, god. Don't remind me. I'm mortified.'

'But what was that all about?' Kitty said. 'It's so unlike you.'

'I don't know,' Sunny said. 'I think part of it was because I knew she was judging me. She looked me up and down the first time she walked in and I knew she was thinking I was repressed in some way, you know? But she's right, I did the same to her.'

'It's like when those workmen shouted at her on the way to the park –' Hannah started.

'I know,' Sunny said. 'You're right. And I'm just as

bad for judging her on her clothes as she is for judging me.'

'And for assuming she's dressing like that for boys,' Kitty said.

Sunny nodded. 'It's so ridiculous. But, yes, everything about her bugged me. How she dressed, how she walked around with her boobs out, how she left her stuff on the floor and made me sleep on the top bunk. So then when I saw her with Will too . . .'

'You flipped,' Hannah said.

'I did,' Sunny said.

23

Sunny hadn't been able to face the zoo. She'd set off with Hannah and Kitty, but her heart wasn't in it. It took her a while to convince them – they said they didn't have to go to the zoo, they were happy to go wherever Sunny wanted – but the zoo wasn't the problem. She was the problem. And she really wanted just to be on her own.

Once they'd gone – making Sunny promise to ring them if she needed them and saying they'd rush right back to find her, wherever she was – Sunny wandered along the Embankment and crossed the bridge towards the fairground.

Sunny stood underneath the Star Flyer – the ride Will had wanted to go on, the ride she said she absolutely wouldn't go on – and looked up. And up. And up. It really was ridiculously high. She couldn't go on it, she really couldn't.

Except she could. There were so many things she

genuinely couldn't do. This thing she could. She was just scared. She walked right up to the window and bought a ticket, her stomach fluttering with nerves and excitement.

While she queued, she tried to switch off her brain. She didn't want to think about Will. Or Danielle. Or moving to London and leaving her friends. Or the course. Or the ride she was about to get on. She just stared at the fence panel next to her and tried to concentrate on her breathing. And then she was at the front and stepping up the metal steps to actually get on the ride and then sitting on the swing and pulling the safety bar across. At the front of the queue the guy had asked how many and she'd told him 'one', assuming everyone else would be in pairs. And she was right. No one came to sit in the empty seat next to her.

It seemed to take forever for everyone to get to their seats and get strapped in and then the staff walked round checking the safety bars, which she was glad of, but she wished they could have done it quicker. She was pretty close to yanking the bar away and making a run for it, but she closed her eyes and made herself stay.

As the seats finally started to rise, she concentrated

on breathing in and out. After rising just a few metres, the ride stopped and Sunny hoped that it was broken and they'd just go back down again and she could get off without being embarrassed because it wasn't her fault. But no. Instead it started to spin. Slowly at first, but then faster, the seats swinging out to the sides. And then it was rising again. She looked down at the fair, wondering if anyone else from the course was there, if they'd see her and wonder why she was on her own, but then she looked out, across the river, across London. And it took her breath away.

It all looked so beautiful, but there was too much to look at, her eyes couldn't take it all in.

The water was shimmering silver and the buildings were glowing gold and then Big Ben started to chime and Sunny felt that bubbling feeling in her belly again. She wasn't sure if it was fear or joy, but it made her eyes fill with tears and it made her laugh out loud.

When Sunny got off the ride she went straight to the back of the queue and waited all over again. She enjoyed the second time even more than the first – this time she knew what to expect and wasn't scared. And didn't waste any of it closing her eyes.

The third time she went on it, Sunny finally remembered the camera in her bag. She took it out and started to film, watching London through the lens. Everything looked slightly different. She noticed things she hadn't seen on the last two rides – boats on the river, the trains crossing the bridges, the food van where she'd got a crêpe with Will . . .

She started to feel a bit dizzy, so she looked up from the camera again and watched the world going round and round.

She thought about moving. About being nearer her family who she loved. About how her dad had been dreaming about the practice with his brother for as long as Sunny could remember. She thought about the boy Aisha liked. She thought about the other film courses she'd seen on the noticeboard at the school. And she thought about how much bigger her life could be. If she was brave. She thought that maybe she could be brave.

24

By the time Sunny got back to the dorm, she was almost giddy with excitement. She wasn't even particularly worried about talking to Danielle. She knew she had to do it and then she could stop worrying and get on with making the film with Hannah, Kitty and Will.

She'd stopped at almost every bench between the South Bank and the dorm and watched the film of the Star Flyer ride over and over again. She'd wanted to go back on it again, but she had to resist. There was something about it, but exactly what she couldn't work out, which is why she wanted to go on again.

As Sunny headed back to the room, the lift pinged and the doors opened to reveal Will.

'Hey!' he said, his face splitting into its huge grin.

'Hi,' Sunny said. She took a deep breath, 'Have you got a minute?'

'For you? I've got all day.'

'Okay,' Sunny said, hearing her voice wobble.

'No, seriously,' Will said. 'I've got nothing to do.'
He pretended to cry. 'I'm so lonely.'

Sunny burst out laughing. 'You're an idiot.'

'Harsh,' he said, grinning again. 'But fair.'

Will pressed the button for the lift and it pinged
and the doors opened again.

'Come with me,' he said to Sunny.

'Um. Where?'

'You'll see. I want to show you something.'

Sunny raised one eyebrow and Will rolled his eyes.
'Not that! Come on.'

Will headed back into the lift and Sunny stepped
in after him. He seemed to press two buttons at once,
but Sunny didn't see which ones. And then the lift set
off.

'It's not going to take off, is it?' she said. 'Like in
Charlie and the Chocolate Factory?'

'I used to have dreams like that,' Will said. 'That
I'd get in a lift, press to go up and the lift would burst
through the roof and go flying off above the buildings.
Sounds cool. Was actually terrifying.'

'Oh no, it definitely sounds more terrifying than
cool,' Sunny said. 'The only recurring dreams I ever
have are where I'm stuck somewhere and trying to
get home, but things keep stopping me. And I can't

make my phone work. And I haven't got any money.'

'Interesting . . .' Will said. 'I think mine's because of –' he gestured at his chair – 'what's yours about, do you reckon?'

'Guilt probably. I feel guilty all the time. About everything.'

'That sounds healthy,' Will said, giving her another one of his smiles. 'Or are you secretly evil?'

Sunny laughed. 'No, not at all evil.' She thought about Danielle. 'Not usually anyway. But I still feel guilty about everything. Like . . . I felt guilty when we couldn't find the disabled ramp for you the other day! Like I was the one who designed the building!'

'Too much empathy, that's your problem,' Will said. 'My mum's a bit like that. Always apologising. She says it's because women are taught to be caretakers and men are taught to be irresponsible.' He raised one eyebrow at Sunny.

She grinned. 'I think my mum would agree with that too.'

The lift stopped at the top floor and the doors opened on to a dingy, grey corridor. Cardboard boxes were piled up along one side and there was a strong smell of mildew.

'Lovely,' Sunny said. 'Do you come here often?'

'Hang on,' Will said. 'And prepare to eat your words.'

Sunny followed him out of the lift and down the corridor towards a blue door covered with warning stickers.

'Are you sure we —' Sunny started.

Will turned the handle and opened the door and Sunny saw that it led out on to the roof.

'Wow!' Sunny gasped.

'See, told you it was good,' Will said.

He wheeled himself through the door and Sunny followed him. The building wasn't exactly a skyscraper so they couldn't see very far over London, but they could see across the rooftops and out to the Shard in the distance. Around the edges of the roof were oblong planters full of flowers.

'Window boxes,' Will said. 'The guy who brought me up here said they used to have them actually at the windows, but one fell off and so they were told they had to get rid of the rest. They brought them up here just to store, planning to get rid of them, but they all just kept growing, so they kept them.'

'Doesn't anyone look after them?' Sunny asked.

'He says not,' Will said. 'But I wouldn't be surprised

if he sneaks up here with a watering can.'

'And a packet of fags,' Sunny said, pointing to a circle of cigarette butts surrounding a metal garden chair in the corner.

'Yeah. Good place to think though,' Will said, wheeling himself over to the edge.

'To think about jumping off?' Sunny asked. Even though the perimeter wall was about up to Sunny's waist, which meant that from his chair Will could barely see over it, her stomach still clenched when he went so close.

'I've spoken to Danielle,' Will said.

Sunny cringed. 'Hang on a sec.'

She crossed the roof and grabbed the metal chair, carrying it over so she was sitting next to Will by the wall.

'I'm sorry I've been such a . . .' She didn't know what word would best describe what she'd been. After a few seconds, she went with, 'An idiot.'

'You haven't,' he said.

'I haven't got a boyfriend,' she told him.

'I know,' he said. 'Danielle told me.'

'Ugh,' Sunny said, looking across at a black-tiled roof broken up with tiny windows. 'Did she tell you I'm a raving bitch?'

'She didn't say "raving" . . .'

Sunny looked at Will. He was smiling, of course.

'So,' Sunny said. And then took a breath to help get the words out. 'You and Danielle, eh?'

Will smiled. 'Yeah. I like her. It's okay that you don't though.'

Sunny shook her head. 'I've realised I don't even know her. If you like her, though, it makes me think I've missed something. I was going to talk to her anyway. I was trying to find her to apologise when I bumped into you.'

'Oh yeah,' Will said, laughing. 'I really had to twist your arm to get you up here. You couldn't get in that lift quick enough!'

'I'm not great at confrontation.' Sunny watched a pigeon fluffing itself up on the roof opposite.

'Who is?' Will said. 'But, you know, if you weren't interested in me, you could've just said.' His mouth quirked at the corner, but Sunny still felt hot with embarrassment.

'It's not that,' she said. 'It's not that I wasn't interested. It's just not . . . something I would do.'

'Because of your parents?' Will asked.

Sunny shook her head. 'No. I mean, that's what I tell people sometimes. Cos it's easier to blame my parents.

But it's just not something I would be interested in. Because of my religion.'

'Right,' Will said, frowning.

'It's my choice!' Sunny said quickly. 'I mean, it's not like Islam forces it on me, or anything. It's my choice not to have a boyfriend.'

Will held his hands up in front of him, palms towards Sunny.

'Sorry,' Sunny said. 'I just don't like it when people make assumptions.'

'Hey,' Will said. 'Look who you're talking to. We've talked about this, right?'

Sunny nodded. 'Yeah. Sorry.'

'You could've just told me. I wasn't planning to leap on you or anything. I thought you were cool – I mean, I still do. You could've just said you weren't looking for lurve.'

Sunny laughed. 'You're right, I'm sorry.'

'And, you know, we've got quite a lot in common. We make a good team.'

'I've always wanted to be on a team,' Sunny said, tugging at the end of her scarf. 'You don't have powers at all, do you?'

Will snorted. 'Wheelchair Boy and Hijab Girl! Fighting crime in the capital!'

'Now that would make a good film,' Sunny said.

Will frowned and then beamed. 'You know what? It really would! We should do that!'

'Fight crime?' Sunny smiled. 'I dunno . . .'

'No, not fight crime, but do something together. Write something, I mean. You know the superhero thing I did on the first day?'

Sunny nodded. 'It was brilliant.'

'I've been thinking about that and I was thinking . . . What would happen to a superhero who got injured? Do they get support from, like, a superheroes' union or something? Or is it just over? They're done.'

'You're thinking of a wheelchair superhero?' Sunny said, leaning forward on her chair.

'Yeah. What do you think?'

Sunny suddenly pictured Will, in a superhero costume, on the Star Flyer and laughed out loud. 'I think it's brilliant.'

25

When Sunny and Will went back downstairs, they found the dorm was mostly quiet – it was a hot day so most of the other students were out and about in London. Miyuki was reading in the common room, her dinosaur backpack on the seat next to her, and Sunny could hear classical music coming from one of the boys' rooms, but it was probably the quietest it had been since they'd arrived.

Will went back to his own room and Sunny took a deep breath as she pushed open the door to the room she shared with Hannah, Kitty and Danielle.

Danielle was sitting in the chair in front of the window – she'd pulled the curtain back and tied it in a knot. She had her laptop on her knee and she was wearing her very ripped jeans with a vest and flip-flops.

She looked up at Sunny, but didn't say anything before returning to her laptop.

'Hey,' Sunny said. 'You're still here.'

''Fraid so,' Danielle said, without looking up.

'I'm glad,' Sunny said.

Danielle did look up then and for a second Sunny felt like she saw a girl her own age.

'Oh yeah?' Danielle said, one eyebrow raised.

Sunny nodded. She crossed the room and stood next to the other window. Even though it was only open a couple of inches because of the locks, the sound of the traffic drifted up.

'Danielle,' Sunny said. 'I owe you an apology.'

Danielle shut the laptop and put it on the desk. 'I owe you one too.'

Sunny frowned. 'Seriously?'

Danielle laughed. 'Yeah? I mean, you were right. I totally judged you as soon as you walked in. I thought you were this meek little Asian girl, you know? Going off to pray all the time, fainting at the sight of my undies. I thought I wouldn't be able to swear in front of you or talk about boys or whatever?'

Sunny smiled. 'I don't think anyone's ever called me meek before.'

'But you were,' Danielle said. 'A bit? I mean, I made you swap beds. And I took your teddy out of its hiding place and you didn't even say. You just sighed and hid it away.'

'I was intimated by you,' Sunny said. 'I mean, if Hannah had hidden Caspar then . . .' She saw Danielle start to smile.

'That's his name!' Sunny said, smiling back. 'If Hannah had done it then I would've just told her to pack it in. But I didn't know you at all. And you were right, we did think we'd have the room to ourselves. We were looking forward to the three of us just hanging out together – we've been friends since primary school – so, yeah, we probably didn't exactly give you the warmest welcome.'

Danielle snorted. 'That's an understatement. It was like walking into a freezer. Steven was warmer when he was bollocking me for setting off the fire alarm.'

'Have you been thrown off the course?' Sunny asked.

Danielle shook her head. 'Well . . . yeah. Officially. But he spoke to my parents and they refused to come and get me, so . . .' She shrugged.

Sunny stared at her. 'Your parents . . . what?'

'They're on holiday,' Danielle said. 'In Italy. That's why I'm here. They offered me a selection of courses and I picked this one cos it was in central London.'

'You didn't want to go to Italy with them?'

Danielle laughed. 'That wasn't one of the options.'

'That's awful!' Sunny said.

'That's why I drink,' Danielle said, and smiled. 'Not really. I didn't want to go with them. I wanted to be in London. And I'm not really surprised they wouldn't come and get me. It's not the first time something like this has happened. I think Steven's a bit traumatised though.'

Sunny didn't know what to say. Once again Danielle had transformed into someone who seemed older, wiser, more cynical, in front of Sunny's eyes.

'I was joking?' Danielle said. 'About the drinking thing? I didn't mean to get drunk. I sometimes have a drink cos it helps me sleep and I just . . . I messed up?'

'Are you . . .' Sunny started, but she wasn't sure exactly how to ask the question she wanted to ask.

'My parents know about it, yeah. And, yes, I've got a "therapist".' She did finger quotes. 'I don't know what happened yesterday really. I'd had a good day. And then we came back here and Will went to bed and no one really wanted to hang out with me and I just felt . . .'

'Lonely?'

'Homesick?' Danielle said. 'I have actually got friends at home, if you can believe that.'

'I can believe it,' Sunny said.

'Two besties,' Danielle said. 'Like you. We do everything together.'

Sunny told Danielle about moving to London. About leaving Kitty and Hannah, having to make all new friends.

'That explains a lot,' Danielle said.

'What?' Sunny frowned.

'Why you were so spiky with me? Cos you're worried about losing your friends and not making new ones? And you wanted to have this time with them and then I came along and buggered it all up?'

Sunny laughed. 'You're good.'

'Therapy,' Danielle said. 'I pick things up.'

They stared at each other for a second and then Sunny said, 'Let me show you something.'

She crossed the room and grabbed the camera out of her bag.

'I've been on that Star Flyer thing at the fair.'

She pulled the chair over next to Danielle's, put the camera on the desk and played the film.

'Woah,' Danielle said. 'That's high.'

'I know,' Sunny said, excitedly. 'But it didn't actually feel that bad once I was up there. It was just amazing. I went on three times and it made me think. About loads of stuff.'

'Like what?' Danielle asked.

On the camera screen, they watched the trains crossing the river on the bridge near the fairground.

'I haven't really thought about it properly yet,' Sunny said. 'So it's probably going to sound stupid . . . But I was thinking of everything as this big thing. My parents want to move down here, right? So I have to move away from my friends and go to a new school and everything. And they talk a lot about me going to university so I've been worrying about that –'

'Already?' Danielle said. 'Jeez.'

'I know. But they want me to do well. And I do too. And I was thinking that I'm going to do medicine like my dad, even though I don't really want to, and it was all this big thing, like a massive weight on my shoulders. But when I got up there and I was looking around, I was thinking . . . it doesn't have to be, does it? The big things are all made up of small things and I can just deal with the small things one at a time.'

She scrolled to a bit of the film showing London from up high, buildings and streets and trains and the river, and then to a bit where she'd zoomed in on the food van.

'You see what I mean?'

'I think so . . .' Danielle said. She looked at Sunny. 'I'm sorry I told Will about your boyfriend.'

'That's okay,' Sunny smiled. 'I'm sorry I made up a boyfriend.'

They both sat back, leaving the camera on the table.

'It's okay for you,' Danielle said, sitting up straighter in her seat. 'You're good at this stuff.' She pointed at the camera. 'You have ideas and you're interested. I thought the course would be, like, making actual films, you know? Not boring background stuff.'

'But next week *is* all about making a film,' Sunny said. 'You've missed most of the boring stuff.'

'And you guys would be okay with me tagging on? When you've done all the boring stuff without me?'

'It's fine with me,' Sunny said. 'And probably with Will too.' She grinned. 'So I'm sure Hannah and Kitty won't mind. But we still have to make the film. Have you got any ideas?'

'I have actually,' Danielle said.

26

'The theme is "conflict",' Mr Berman said, sitting on the desk at the front of the room. 'And it is up to you to interpret that as you wish.'

Sunny glanced at Danielle, who was sitting on her right. Danielle winked and Sunny laughed.

'The only conditions,' Mr Berman said, 'are that you must demonstrate the different skills and techniques you've learned on the course. There has to be a story. It doesn't have to be fiction – documentary is fine – but there needs to be a beginning, a middle, an end and a point. If anyone needs any help or advice, you know where I am.'

They spent the rest of the morning watching the previous year's short films, which were brilliant and intimidating. Sunny's favourite was a sci-fi rom-com that reminded her of the thoughts she'd had about the alien taxi when they'd been on their way to meet Tom the previous week.

'So what do you think?' Danielle said.

They had the afternoon free to brainstorm film ideas, so they'd decided to go to the Rainforest Café for lunch with discount vouchers they'd been given by a guy in Covent Garden piazza.

'I love it,' Kitty said.

'I don't know how I didn't think of it,' Sunny said, shaking her head.

Danielle laughed. 'You mean how come I thought of it instead of you?'

'No, I didn't mean that!' Sunny said. 'I mean . . . I talked about it. To Kitty.'

'I was just kidding,' Danielle said. 'So, how are we going to do it?'

'Hang on,' Will said. He was sitting at the end of the oblong table because of his wheelchair. He held his hand up to the others and pointed at a gorilla standing in the foliage on the other side of the room.

'This again?' Hannah said.

'It moved!' Will said. 'I'm telling you.'

Danielle pretended to sniff his drink.

'Just wait,' Will insisted.

They all silently watched the gorilla, but nothing happened. And then the waiter arrived and took their food order.

'So, how do we do it?' Danielle said again.

'People shout stuff at you, right?' Sunny asked Danielle.

'Oh yeah,' Danielle said. 'Men mostly. Although sometimes girls call me a slag.'

'Ugh,' Sunny said. 'Well, we could go somewhere and see if anyone shouts something and then film that or –'

'It doesn't have to be real,' Will said. 'It could be a docu-drama. We could recreate the kind of things that happen, the things people say.'

'That's what I was going to say,' Sunny said.

'Sorry,' Will smiled.

'So we'd do people shouting stuff at me and then at you,' Danielle asked Sunny.

Sunny nodded.

'And then what?' Hannah asked.

They all looked at each other.

'It just moved!' Will shouted.

'Then how come none of us saw it?' Sunny said, grinning at the others.

'Ah,' Will said. 'You're winding me up.'

The other four laughed.

'That's great,' Will said. 'Mock the disabled.'

'Oh, shut up,' Sunny grinned. 'Yes. It turns its head

every couple of minutes – how could you think we wouldn't have seen it?'

'I'm shocked and appalled,' Will said.

'We could use some newspaper headlines,' Danielle suggested. 'Or we could find stuff online? Articles about how awful it is that Muslim women are "forced to cover up". Articles about how women who dress like me have no self-respect?'

'That would work,' Sunny said.

'And we could do some vox pops,' Hannah said. 'We could ask people what they think of how Sunny's dressed and what they think about how you're dressed, Danielle.'

'And what you said yesterday,' Kitty said to Sunny. 'About how much is okay? You wear too much, Danielle doesn't wear enough. What's the right amount?'

'Exactly!' Sunny and Danielle said at the same time.

'Look at you two,' Hannah said. 'You're not . . . friends?'

'Stranger things have happened,' Danielle said, grinning.

'That reminds me,' Will said. 'You know Sophie? When they chucked us all out on Saturday night, she wasn't in her room.'

'Shut up,' Sunny said. 'Where was she?' She really couldn't imagine Sophie breaking any rules.

'She was with Cameron.'

'That annoying short boy?' Hannah said. 'Wow.'

'Yep,' Will nodded. 'She's gone home now, I think. Her parents were coming for her today. Cameron's too.'

'Wow,' Sunny said. 'How did you find out?'

'Oh,' Will said. 'Well. Yeah, that's probably something I should tell you. Since we're bonding and everything.'

They all stared at him, waiting for him to speak.

'Liz?' he said. 'The chaperone? She's my mum.'

'Shut up,' Hannah said.

'No, I'm serious,' Will said. 'I made her promise not to say anything because, well, you know, as if I wanted people to think I'd brought my mum with me.'

'That makes sense,' Kitty said.

'Are she and Steven . . . ?' Hannah said.

'What?' Will said, frowning. 'Oh god! No! I don't think so anyway. God. What made you ask that?!'

'Oh I just got a bit of a . . . vibe,' Hannah said.

'God,' Will said again. 'So I'll be asking her about that then.'

'That's not why she's there though, is it?' Sunny said. 'It's her job, right?'

Will nodded. 'Yeah. She's done it a few times now. But it's like being the teacher's kid, isn't it? No one wants that. Specially when people already make assumptions about me cos of the chair.'

They sat in silence for few seconds, Will frowning and shaking his head, and then he said 'Hey!' and smacking the edge of the table with both hands.

'We know,' Sunny said. 'The gorilla moves. Let it go.'

'No,' Will said. 'I was just thinking that maybe we could expand on the film ideas. Sort of. You can't judge a book by its cover – people make assumptions about Danielle cos of how she dresses. And you because of your headscarf. And me because of my chair.'

'Yes!' Sunny said. 'That could work.'

'And Kitty's gay,' Hannah said.

'You're gay?' Danielle said. 'For real?'

Kitty nodded, her cheeks pink.

'And I'm the slapper,' Hannah said, just as a waiter appeared and gave her a disapproving look.

They all laughed.

'So when do we start?' Danielle said.

27

'Maybe it wouldn't be so bad if you moved down here,' Kitty said as they walked back through Leicester Square towards the dorm. Will and Danielle had gone to the cinema.

Sunny stared at her. 'But I'd miss you so much!'

'I'd miss you too!' Kitty said, hooking her arm through Sunny's. 'But I just think you might be really happy here. You talk about your family a lot. And you were talking about coming here for university. You're just getting on with it a bit sooner, that's all.'

'I know,' Sunny said. 'I've been thinking the same thing. It's just happening so fast. I thought we'd have another few years of all being idiots together!'

'Me and Hannah can come down for idiot weekends,' Kitty said.

'That would be ace,' Sunny said.

'Have you talked to your dad?' Hannah asked Sunny.

Sunny shook her head. 'I've texted, but I haven't spoken to him.'

'You've been avoiding him?' Kitty asked.

'Little bit, yeah,' Sunny said, dodging a group of tourists gathered round a guide holding a rainbow-striped umbrella.

'God, Sun, that's not like you,' Hannah said.

'I know. I just . . . I had lots of stuff I wanted to think about, you know?' Sunny said. 'And Dad's always so enthusiastic about everything.'

'Oh yeah. He's awful,' Kitty said, grinning.

'You know what I mean,' Sunny said. 'Your dad's just the same.'

'Yep,' Kitty said. 'You need to sit him down and really talk to him. Tell him what you're worried about. He'll understand, I'm sure. He's fab.'

'Yeah, he is,' Sunny said.

'What time are you calling Jack?' Sunny asked Kitty as they walked up the stairs to their room.

'He said to call him whenever,' Kitty said. 'We could ring him now? And then we'll have stuff to tell Will and Danielle when they get back?'

'Great,' Sunny said, at the top of the stairs. 'I'm just going to get a drink.'

Along the corridor, Sunny could hear music and TV coming from people's rooms and the low hum of chatter and laughter that always seemed to be the sound of the dorm. She pushed open the door to the kitchen and saw her dad.

He was sitting at the long table in front of the coffee machine. He looked so out of place that at first she couldn't quite take in what she was seeing. She opened and closed her mouth without managing to make a sound and it was only when he stood up and walked towards her that she recovered.

'Hey!' Sunny said. 'What are you doing here?' She thought for a second that he'd come to take her home and she realised she really didn't want to go. Not yet. 'What's wrong?' she said. 'Is something wrong? Is Mum okay?'

'Your mum's fine,' he said, putting his hands on her shoulders and kissing her on the forehead. 'Nothing to worry about.'

'Why are you here?' Sunny said. 'What's –'

'I said there's nothing to worry about,' he said. 'I just wanted to see my daughter and take her out for a cup of tea. Okay?'

'Okay,' Sunny said.

She followed him back towards the stairs. She felt completely disoriented. She'd have to text Kitty and Hannah and tell them where she was. When she got there. Wherever they were going.

Her dad didn't say anything on the way down – Sunny could hear him humming under his breath, which he always did when he was thinking. It was only when they were on the street outside that he stopped and turned to her.

'You haven't phoned.'

Sunny's throat felt tight with tears. 'I'm sorry,' she managed to squeak out.

'We'll talk more in Starbucks,' he said. 'Is Starbucks okay?'

Sunny nodded. As they walked along the Strand, she felt self-conscious. She was trying hard not to cry and, walking quickly to keep up with her much taller father, she felt like a child. Which she supposed she was. She had started to feel so different in London on her own, it was strange to be her dad's daughter again. They stopped to cross a road and her dad reached for her hand. She felt better as soon as she let him take it – his huge, warm, familiar hand, holding hers to guide her across the road. She started breathing properly again.

'You promise it's nothing bad?' she said.

He stopped and turned to her. 'Oh, Sunshine. It's nothing bad.' He hugged her, resting his chin on her head and moving his jaw from side to side, which he knew really annoyed her. It made her feel so much better.

He opened the door to Starbucks and ushered her inside before him. 'You go and sit,' he said. 'Hot chocolate?'

Sunny nodded and headed to the furthest point of the café, which, she noticed, thinking of Will, was down a step. She sat down and watched her dad at the counter. She thought about the film and tried to imagine, if she didn't know him, what she would think about him. He was wearing slightly too loose jeans – he always bought a bigger size because he said he wanted to be comfortable – and his long-sleeved T-shirt was a bit raggedy and shapeless, but he looked nice. He was chatting to the barista, a big smile on his face, and something about him just suggested that he was kind. Sunny had an urge to cross the café and give him a hug, but decided to wait until he came over to the table.

'So,' he said, putting down a hot chocolate and a big slice of cake.

'So, I can't eat that,' Sunny said.

His eyebrows shot up. 'Are you ill?'

Sunny laughed. 'No! I've been eating all day.'

He shrugged. 'Then there's no harm in having some more.'

'You're a doctor!' Sunny said, laughing.

He sat down, grinning at her. 'I know you love cake. I like to make you happy.'

'Stand up again a minute,' Sunny said.

'Why?'

Sunny stood up next to him. 'Just do it!'

Her dad stood up and she hugged him around his waist. He wrapped his arms around her and squeezed. And then they both sat down again.

'What was that for?' he asked.

'I just really missed you,' she said. 'And I love you.'

'I love you too,' he said. 'Your mum wanted me to come and bring you home. She was so mad.'

Sunny pulled a face.

'But I said no. I said we can trust our Sunny. I knew you were just being independent and having fun. But that you'd be responsible.'

'I was,' Sunny said. 'I am.'

'But also I think we need to talk about Sam?'

'Sam?' Sunny said. The fluttery feeling was back in her stomach again.

'From your school? We saw him one day in town. In the bookshop, you know? The cheap one?'

Sunny nodded.

'He came over to talk to us. He asked if we'd heard from you, how you were getting on, when you were back. He said you'd been texting him, but you'd stopped.'

Sunny nodded.

'You were texting him?' her dad said.

'Yes. He's a friend,' Sunny said. 'I mean, I think he likes me. But there's nothing going on. I just . . . he's funny. He stood up for me at school when some boy was saying stuff about me. And he was nice to Kitty when all that stuff happened with Dylan.'

'That's fine,' her dad said. 'We just weren't sure. He was very familiar . . .'

Sunny smiled. 'He's just like that. He's sort of like a puppy.'

Her dad laughed. 'Yes. So there's nothing I need to know?'

'Dad! God. No.'

'And no one here I need to know about?'

'There's a boy in our group on the course – Will – but he's just a friend too. You know that. You know I'd never –'

Her dad shook his head. 'I know, I know. You're a good girl.' He pushed the cake towards her. 'Eat some cake.'

'No,' Sunny said, pushing the plate away. 'I need to talk to you about something.'

'Go ahead,' her dad said.

Sunny took a breath. Then she pulled the cake back towards her and shoved a forkful in her mouth. Once she'd swallowed it, she said, 'I don't think I want to study medicine.'

Her dad looked confused. Sunny could feel her heart pounding. She listened to the hiss of the coffee machine and stared down at the cake crumbs on the plate in front of her.

'I don't think I want you to study medicine either!' her dad said. 'Did you think I did?'

Sunny looked up at him. 'Yes! Don't you? I mean, you used to talk about me joining the practice!'

Her dad's eyes widened. 'Years ago! When you were a little girl! It was a joke. Have you been worrying about this?'

Sunny nodded. 'A little bit, yeah.'

Her dad shook his head. 'No no no. I think medicine would be too much stress for you. I know how conscientious you are. You worry too much. You would take it all on and it would be awful for you.'

'Okay,' Sunny said, frowning. She wanted more cake.

'Your mum and I just want you to be happy.'

'That's not true!' Sunny said. 'You want me to be successful! If I said I'd decided not to go to uni and I was going to, I don't know, sell crafts in the market or something . . . You wouldn't be okay with that!'

'No. Because neither would you! You've always been ambitious and dedicated. Even since you were a little girl. We worried about you because you never coloured outside the lines!' He laughed. 'You were always so careful.'

'I'd like to think about doing something with film,' Sunny said. 'I mean, I know I've only done a week of this course and I know it's ages until I go to uni, but I want you to know that that's what I'm thinking right now. And I want to know if it's okay with you.'

'It's absolutely fine with me, Sanari. And it will be fine with your mother too.'

Sunny couldn't quite speak yet, so she just nodded. Her dad hardly ever called her by her proper name – she could barely remember the last time.

'So, do you have a film to show me?' her dad asked.

'No,' Sunny said, swallowing. 'But I will next week.'

'Excellent!' He grinned. And took a bite of Sunny's cake.

28

'I think we need to cut the introduction,' Will said, scrolling up on the screen and highlighting the first two paragraphs.

Sunny pretended to scream. They'd spent ages working on the introduction, then cut it and put it back in.

'I think it gives the point away,' Will said. 'We want them to realise what it's about, not be told right up front.'

'I agree,' Hannah said. 'We could always spell it out at the end if we think people won't get it, but I don't think we should begin with it.'

When Sunny, Kitty and Hannah had spoken to Jack, he'd told them that knowing what they wanted to say was more important than how they said it, so they'd been working on the script all day before starting filming the following day. They'd spent the morning in the studio, but moved to the girls' room in the afternoon because they'd started to find the studio claustrophobic. Also, there were snacks in the dorm kitchen with a note from Liz saying to help themselves.

The following day, they walked down to Victoria Embankment Gardens to do some vox pops. They let Danielle take the lead because she'd been so good at getting people to talk before.

'No running off today though,' Hannah said as they walked between the beds of enormous tropical plants.

Danielle shook her head. 'Definitely not. I'm sorry about that.' She ducked as a pigeon flew up in front of her. 'You lot were all just so . . . cosy together.' She grinned. 'It was kind of sickening. But I still shouldn't have left.'

'And we should have noticed,' Sunny said.

'Wait,' Danielle said, stopping and looking at them. 'You didn't even notice?!'

Towards the exit, they found a sectioned-off area with a small stage and deck chairs set out in circles.

'It looks just like the pier at home!' Sunny said, flopping backwards into one of the deck chairs. 'And these things are just as uncomfortable.'

Danielle had perched herself on the side of Will's

wheelchair, and he had his arm around her waist. Sunny looked at them and realised she didn't feel anything. Not embarrassment, not anger, certainly not jealousy. She hoped they'd keep in touch, and not just because they'd be her only friends down South.

29

The screening of the final videos was much more relaxed than it had been in the original competition. For one, they had nothing to lose – it would be nice to win Best Film, but it was no big deal if they didn't.

The best thing about it was that it was taking place in a preview cinema in Golden Square. The cinema only had about eighty seats, but Steven had told everyone to get dressed up and he was wearing a tuxedo, so it almost felt like a proper premiere. The atmosphere in the dorm was fabulous. Once everyone was dressed, they all left their doors open and, for the first time since the start of the course, everyone was milling in and out of each other's rooms.

'We should have been doing this all along!' Hannah said.

She was drinking fruit punch from a jam jar.

'You've got a great view,' Miyuki said. She was

wearing a dress patterned with teacups, but still had her dinosaur backpack on over the top.

'Yeah,' Sunny said. 'I'm going to miss it.'

Sunny rested her head against the window. She felt like recording the sound of the traffic so she could listen to it at bedtime at home and pretend she was still here. But maybe the new house would be noisy. She was sort of looking forward to seeing it.

Danielle came over and said, 'I love that sound.'

'Me too,' Sunny said.

'At home, we live out in the country. All I ever hear is birds. I didn't think I'd be able to sleep here at first, but now I'm not sure I'll be able to sleep at home?'

'I was just thinking the same thing,' Sunny said.

'You look nice,' Danielle said.

Sunny was wearing a hijab and a tunic top with loose cream trousers and her black ballet slippers. She laughed. 'Do you think?'

'You do!' Danielle said. 'But . . . what size shoe are you?'

'I don't wear heels,' Sunny said quickly.

'No, not heels. What about my gold sandals?'

Sunny bit the inside of the corner of her mouth. 'Which are they?'

Danielle hooked them out from under the bed. They were flat, Roman-style sandals. Strappy but relatively comfy-looking. Sunny frowned.

'They're fine,' Danielle said. 'I haven't got, like, verrucas or anything.'

'No, it's not that . . .' Sunny said. 'It's just . . . isn't it a bit blee wearing someone else's shoes?'

Danielle shook her head. 'Maybe. I don't know. You don't have to, I just thought they'd look nice on you, that's all.'

Sunny looked down at her feet and then at Danielle's shoes. And then at Danielle. She was wearing a skintight striped dress with lacy panels down the sides and high-heeled shoes that tied at the ankles with ribbons.

'Can I just try them on?' Sunny said. She sat down on the chair by the desk and pulled the shoes over towards her. She put them on and looked down. Danielle was right – they did look good.

'What do you think?' she called over to Hannah and Kitty.

Kitty was wearing a top quite similar to Danielle's dress, but with cropped black trousers and red ballet shoes. Hannah was wearing a red dress with a full skirt and ankle boots. They both looked great.

'They look amazing!' Hannah said.

'Did you bring any earrings?' Kitty said.

'Duh,' Sunny said. She'd forgotten to put them on. 'Are you sure it's okay if I wear them?' she asked Danielle.

'Course. I offered didn't I?'

Sunny went to the bathroom and got her gold hoop earrings out of her washbag. She put them on and then added a bit more lip gloss then smiled at herself in the mirror. She actually had butterflies. It wasn't even as if she was going to a real premiere, but the atmosphere in the dorm was buzzing. Just as she came out of the loo, Will came in, using his stick.

'Wit woo!' he said, grinning.

'Wit woo yourself.' She smiled back. He was wearing black trousers and a white shirt over a Superman T-shirt.

'Are you all ready to go?' he asked.

'Think so,' Sunny said.

He held his arm out to her. 'Fancy escorting me downstairs?'

Sunny nodded.

'Meet you in the lobby?' she said to the girls.

'We're on our way,' Hannah replied.

'So when you move down here . . .' Will said in the lift. 'Maybe we could meet up sometime? In town, I mean?'

Sunny smiled. 'I'd like that.'

'I think we work pretty well together. Maybe we could do another film project.'

Sunny nodded. 'Definitely. I think the world needs Wheelchair Boy and Hijab Girl.'

Hannah, Kitty, Danielle and Miyuki were already in the lobby when Sunny and Will got there.

'Have you seen what's outside?' Hannah said.

They pushed the door open to find a stretch limo on the street outside.

'Oh my god!' Sunny said, running out on to the street and almost tripping over Danielle's sandals. 'I've always wanted to go in one of these!'

'There are two,' Miyuki said. 'Steven told me. They have to keep coming back for us all so we've got to wait in Golden Square until everyone arrives.'

'Is there something to do there?' Hannah asked.

'There's a park in the middle. It's nice in the sun.' Miyuki shrugged.

'Can we just get in it?' Danielle said.

'I think so,' Will said.

Danielle opened the car door and jumped straight in, followed by Will.

It was dark inside the limo, lit with blue strip lighting across the top of the windows.

'No bar?' Danielle said.

'We're fourteen!' Sunny said, laughing.

'You might be,' Danielle said. 'I'm fifteen.' She flopped back on her seat. 'This is the life.'

A couple more students got in and the driver set off.

'Can we stand up through the roof?' Hannah said, pressing a button. Nothing happened.

'The roof doesn't open,' a voice said through a small speaker.

'Damn,' Danielle said. 'We'll just have to open the windows then.'

The windows did open and they all took turns poking their heads out. Sunny held on to her hijab with both hands and tried to take it all in and remember exactly how she felt. She wanted to remember it for the rest of her life. She was in a limo, with her friends, on the way to a film premiere. A fake one, but even so.

They all cheered as they reached Piccadilly Circus and everyone squeezed out of the windows together.

They waved at the tourists standing on the steps around Eros and Sunny pulled her phone out to try to take a selfie, but she couldn't get her arm out far enough without worrying a passing car would knock it out of her hand.

The limo dropped them in front of a dark brown building that looked like something from Sherlock.

'No way!' Kitty said, suddenly. She opened the limo door and almost fell out on to the side of the road.

'What's up with her?' Hannah said.

Sunny peered out of the door and then grinned. 'Dylan's here.'

They all crossed over into Golden Square. Dylan and Kitty sat down on the grass, holding hands and nuzzling each other, while the rest of them wandered around or sat in the sun.

When the last limo of students arrived, the doors of the building opened and a woman in a white dress and knee-high red boots ushered them inside. It just seemed like an ordinary office building until she showed them into the screening room, which was entirely red — red walls, red carpet, red seats. There were old-fashioned red-and-white striped cardboard boxes of popcorn tucked into the arm of each seat and milk bottles of lemonade with red-and-white paper straws on the other side.

'How cool is this?' Kitty said.

Sunny hugged her. 'It's so brilliant.'

They all sat down on the front row and Miyuki took a photo of them. Then they took one of her and then they all texted the photos to each other.

Once everyone was finally seated, Steven stood at the front and talked about how brilliant the course had been, how impressed he was with the way everyone had worked. He said they'd had to deal with some challenging situations – here he looked at Danielle – but he was happy with how everything had been handled and more than proud of the finished films.

And then the lights went down.

After a few false starts, Sunny, Kitty, Hannah, Danielle and Will had ended up filming themselves and the other students against a black background, everyone talking about their first impressions of each other. In between each person talking, they'd shown the vox pops, along with clips from newspaper headlines, magazine articles and online comments.

They hadn't needed the introduction or a conclusion, the film completely spoke for itself.

Sunny had watched it dozens of times over the last couple of days, but it gave her goose bumps every time.

30

On the tube to Euston, Sunny looked at herself in the dark window opposite. She looked the same, but she felt different. She was so proud of the film they'd made. It hadn't won 'Best Film' – a thriller about a boy doing parkour through King's Cross station had won that – but it had won 'Most Thought-provoking' and Sunny was happy with that.

The man sitting next to her shifted in his seat and she glanced at him. He had a tattoo of Big Bird from Sesame Street on his arm. Sunny grinned and tried to point it out to Hannah, who was sitting opposite, without actually talking or indeed pointing. Hannah just frowned at her and mouthed, 'What?'

Kitty and Dylan hadn't been able to get seats, but they didn't seem concerned. They were standing at the end of the carriage, leaning back against the bit of seat stuck to the wall for that purpose. They were talking and smiling and, as Sunny watched, Dylan kissed Kitty on her temple and Kitty threaded her fingers through Dylan's.

Sunny knew she was going to miss them all so much.

As they stood looking up at the huge wall of departure boards at Euston, Sunny realised something.

'You know next time I'm here, I'll probably be coming up to visit you, not going home,' she said.

Kitty flung an arm around her. 'I still can't believe you're actually moving away. I'm going to miss you so much.'

'But we're going to visit,' Hannah said. 'Definitely. You'll probably get sick of us.'

'Never,' Sunny said, smiling at Dylan over the top of Kitty's head.

The thought of moving away gave Sunny butterflies, but they were butterflies of excitement rather than fear. It was a whole new beginning.

And she was ready.

Acknowledgements

This book probably wouldn't exist without Lily Webber. Thank you for the idea, the film course info, and your enthusiasm, Lily.

Thank you to my fabulous agent, Hannah Sheppard, and wonderful editor, Liz Bankes, both of whom make writing books less painful and more fun.

Thank you to Tim Rose for another wonderful cover.

Thank you to Iffath Ahmed and Fatima Patel for answering my many (and often stupid) questions. And to Gila Groger and Emma McCann for info about Hypermobility Syndrome (http://hypermobility. org/) and being a part-time wheelchair user. Any mistakes are my own, of course.

Thank you to Amber Kirk-Ford for the high five joke that I totally nicked off Twitter and to Steven Perkins for letting me use his name, not that I asked.

Gentle hugs to Claire Bentley, Caroline Clarke, Allie Dickinson, Carrie Dunn, Alexandra Roumbas Goldstein, Eve Harvey, Jenni Nock and Kelly Railton.

Thank you to my wonderful writer friends who inspire me, support me, and make me cry with laughter on a daily basis. Calming manatees to you all. Extra thanks to Susie Day for the South Bank convo that made this book so much better.

An all caps THANK YOU to everyone who reads and raves about UKYA in general and my books in particular. You're the BEST.

Finally, thank you to David for working so hard, cooking every night and taking the boys away when I need to get on with some work; to Harry for being sweet and hilarious and occasionally making me a much-needed cup of tea; and to Joe for being the best at killing the Ender Dragon (and suggesting his own acknowledgement). I love you all muchly.

Praise for STARRING KITTY

'A novel that stands out for the realistic and touching quality of the teenage relationships.' *The Telegraph*

'If you know a 10-14 human who likes things that are good, please give them this book.' Susie Day

'Kitty is a fantastic heroine, quiet but creative and brave . . . this is a FABULOUS book.' Stephanie Burgis

'It's complicated . . . Kitty's life, that is. I was rooting for her all the way!' Karen McCombie

'Without huge drama or major issues being signposted or thrust down people's throats, it just gently gets on with being what it is: a straightforward and very sweet story about first love. We need more books like this out there.' Liz Kessler

'Starring Kitty is pretty much one of the best books you could ever wish to read, and I don't ever say that lightly.' Queen of Contemporary

'This book is such a sweet and lovely story that it felt like a cuddle in a warm blanket in book form.' Sister Spooky.

'Perfect mood-busting book which I read with a huge smile on my face right the way through.' YA Yeah Yeah

'Bravo to Keris and Catnip for this wonderful little book which is heartfelt and gorgeous throughout. I cannot wait for the rest of the series.' The Overflowing Library